"Olivia Monroe killed her first husband then jumped into bed with her boss, the richest married rat in town!"

Olivia and Nat stood behind the man as he continued to make the scandalous allegations. "Ask anyone—she's been sleeping with my big brother for years, and it's not going to stop just because she's got herself a solid gold meal ticket for life, all legally tied up with wedding lines!"

DIANA HAMILTON is a true romantic at heart and fell in love with her husband at first sight. They still live in the fairy-tale Tudor house where they raised their three children. Now the idyll is shared with eight rescued cats and a puppy. But despite an often chaotic life-style, ever since she learned to read and write Diana has had her nose in a book— either reading or writing one—and plans to go on doing just that for a very long time to come.

Books by Diana Hamilton

Don't miss any of our special offers. Write to us at the following address for information on our newest releases.

Harlequin Reader Service
U.S.: 3010 Walden Ave., P.O. Box 1325, Buffalo, NY 14269
Canadian: P.O. Box 609, Fort Erie, Ont. L2A 5X3

DIANA HAMILTON

Scandalous Bride

Harlequin Books

TORONTO • NEW YORK • LONDON
AMSTERDAM • PARIS • SYDNEY • HAMBURG
STOCKHOLM • ATHENS • TOKYO • MILAN
MADRID • WARSAW • BUDAPEST • AUCKLAND

ISBN 0-373-11936-4

SCANDALOUS BRIDE

First North American Publication 1998.

Copyright © 1997 by Diana Hamilton.

CHAPTER ONE

'OLIVIA MONROE killed her first husband then jumped into bed with her boss, the richest married rat in town!'

The male voice, thick with alcohol, penetrated the smoochy dance music and the nightclub chatter. Olivia stiffened in Nathan's arms, flinching as she heard a woman shriek, 'You can't be serious, Hughie!'

'Ask anyone—she's been sleeping with my big brother for years and it's not going to stop just because she's got herself a solid gold meal-ticket for life, all legally tied up with wedding lines!'

'The Olivia who married that scrummy, rich as a plum-cake Nathan Monroe? Their wedding made the front pages a couple of months ago—good grief! Does he know he's been taken for a sucker?' The woman was obviously loving every minute of it and Olivia felt sick, her feet rooting themselves to the minute dance-floor. The elegant, glittering surroundings suddenly felt tawdry.

Had Nathan heard?

Nathan had.

His big, hard body went still. He took an incisive step back, his arms falling to his sides as his hands made dangerous fists. She looked up into his harsh and beautiful face and shuddered, her skin crawling with fire and then ice.

Sometimes the inescapable intensity of what she felt for him frightened her. The inadmissible knowledge that she couldn't live without him, the way her blood turned to a burning torrent when he walked into a room, the reckless way she'd given every last scrap of her future happiness into his keeping when, years ago, she'd solemnly and sensibly vowed she would never fall in love again.

And now the anger frightened her. Savage, black anger blazing in those steel-grey eyes, pulling the tanned flesh tight against his strong and elegant bones.

Instinctively, her eyes sifted through the swaying bodies, homing in on Hugh Caldwell. Running to fat, he looked older than his thirty-four years. For a split second her eyes clashed with his, dark brown and malicious, before he led his dance partner off the floor with a smirk on his dissolute face.

Olivia held her breath, shocked by the vile gossip Hugh was spreading. The sound of the music had faded, the noise people made when they were enjoying themselves ebbing out of her consciousness, and all she could hear was the thunderous beat of her heart and Nathan's ice-cold threat, 'I'll kill the son of a bitch!'

'Don't.' Her hand on the black sleeve of his dinner jacket stayed him. He swung round to face her, his shoulders wide and hard, intimidating. She took a deep breath. One of them had to remain cool and collected. She felt anything but. However, she'd spent long, lonely years perfecting her act.

'Make a scene and you'll give credence to his foul lies,' she advised quickly. 'Think about it.'

Of all the exclusive nightclubs in London why had Hugh Caldwell chosen this one? He'd been born with a chip on his shoulder and for the past thirty-four years it had been growing heavier by the day. She had always suspected he could be dangerous but hadn't imagined he could stoop so low. The cold premonition of disaster feathered over her skin, making her shiver, but—

'Ignore him, or sue. Or both,' she said calmly, her mind frantically willing him to agree. He looked capable of tearing Hugh Caldwell limb from limb and taking savage pleasure from every moment.

She hated violence in any form. For one terrible day, the last day of her first husband's life, she had known what physical violence really was. She had known that it had fatally poisoned their already weakened relationship and had opened her eyes to the fact that violence of another form, emotional violence, had been eroding their marriage almost from day one. 'Don't put yourself down on his level.'

That, mercifully, appeared to have the desired effect. She actually saw the battle to rein in his flaring anger. And saw him win. But then nothing ever defeated him, did it? She fought her own impulse to sag with relief, simply dipping her head coolly as he commanded, tight-lipped, 'We're leaving.'

And she walked out at his side, five feet three inches of dignity, her glossy black hair whispering against the tanned skin of her back where the sweeping cut of the elegant white dress left it bare. Her amethyst eyes were staring straight ahead and her sultry mouth was caught tight against her teeth in case the tremor of her lips gave her away.

But distressed tremors plagued her on the taxi ride back to the Chelsea mews cottage and she couldn't relax enough to make them stop.

'It's cute,' he'd said when he'd snapped the cottage up just days before their wedding. 'A London base for a time. I haven't had a permanent home in England for years. A cute and private place to make memories before we move on. Like it, sweetheart?'

She'd loved it on sight. Loved the dolls' house proportions, the cosy, secluded atmosphere, projecting that love into the wonderful memories they'd make together, not heeding the warnings about moving on, not even hearing them properly.

But now he wasn't saying a thing. The distance between them was far more than a few feet of upholstery. The tension between them was making the small space a void.

He was a proud man with a streak of self-assurance a whole mile wide. A hard man. A brilliant wheeler-dealer, a key stock-market player, his mind had the cutting edge of a diamond.

No one took him for a ride, called him a sucker. That taunt would be eating up his mind. Perhaps even more than the evil slur on her character.

Olivia ached to touch him but didn't dare. The dam would burst soon enough and the back of a London cab wasn't the place to cope with it.

If only they'd stayed home tonight, she agonised futilely. But they'd been on the verge of their very first fight. One week back at work after their idyllic two-month honeymoon in the Bahamas, he had as good as demanded she hand in her resignation. He'd wanted to know why she hadn't already done just that, and she had tried to explain her reluctance, put forward her own ideas, both of them getting more uptight by the moment until he'd pulled them away from the danger with that mind-shatteringly wicked grin of his.

'Forget it, for now. We'll eat out tonight, somewhere special. And go clubbing afterwards. Celebrate being married for two months and a week.' His steely eyes had warmed in that special way, for her alone, and her insides had capered about, twisting with love for him as she'd hurried to change with no foreknowledge of how the evening would end...

After the taxi had drawn away the mews was quiet, the single street lamp accentuating the black shadows. Nathan opened the front door, de-activated the alarm system and stood aside, allowing her to walk through to the cottage-style sitting room in front of him. His silence and the tight cast of his features were ominous.

She switched on a parchment-shaded table lamp, dousing the main lights, preferring the subdued effect. The soft glow made the cottage antiques and the squashily upholstered twin sofas seem so safe and cosy—a much needed antidote to the arctic chill of the atmosphere Nathan was generating.

'Were they foul lies?' His voice abraded her.

A give-away flicker of pain darkened her eyes, but only a flicker; she had it under control even though she felt she was coming part, her flesh being painfully stripped from her bones by the knife-edge of his lack of trust.

'How can you even ask?' Her voice was cool, masking her desperate hurt, her body in the under-statedly sexy white dress taut and slim and proud. 'Don't you know me better than that—well enough to make the asking of such a question totally irrelevant and completely offensive?'

She lifted her chin higher, blanking out the shame-ful, hateful knowledge that not all of Hugh's mali-cious gossip had been lies, and felt the deep ache of misery spread right through her as he answered tersely, 'I only know what you choose to tell me.'

He turned his back on her, moving to a side table and sloshing two inches of malt whisky into a glass, draining it in one swallow, his mouth tight as he re-minded her, 'We saw each other, were poleaxed and were married three weeks later.' He dragged in a sharp breath, his eyes holding hers, adding more slowly, 'I never thought such a thing could happen to me.'

His lips curled wryly at the memory of that cata-clysmic happening and her body leapt in ferocious response at the wonderful memories: the way they hadn't been able to keep their hands off each other, the way they hadn't been able to handle being apart, the glorious, fated inevitability of it all.

But then they were dragged back to the present, the brief bonding of shared and precious memories over.

'Apart from the information that you are an only child and that your parents separated, I know two hard facts about your past,' he stated. 'First, you married when you were nineteen, his name was Max and he died six years later. Second, as a widow you became married to your career and that lasted for three years, until we met,' he enumerated harshly.

'Or am I wrong there? Does your career still come first? Is that why you won't quit?' His face tightened. 'My work takes me all over the world—you know that. I want you with me, not stuck back here—you know that, too. Is being a PA to the head of Caldwell Engineering more important to you than being with me? Or does the attraction lie mainly with your boss, rather than the job itself?'

Olivia shivered uncontrollably, despising herself for that small betrayal. They had come full circle, right back to where the disastrous evening had started. But, worse than that, he had taken the gossip on board, beginning to question her relationship with her boss, James Caldwell.

She watched numbly as he dragged his black tie away from his shirt, tossing it onto one of the sofas, his jacket following a scant second later. And then he turned and met her wide and wounded eyes.

Even as he held her gaze his expressive mouth softened. His brow furrowing, he dragged taut fingers through his midnight-dark hair. 'God, I'm sorry, Livvy. Come here.'

She went into his arms willingly, as she always would, the inescapable tug of the wicked chemistry that had sprung to inexorable life between them the moment they'd met working its unending magic.

His arms enfolded her with savage passion, pulling her slender curves into his hard, lean frame, his voice thick and raw with contrition as he bent his dark head and covered her neck with scalding kisses. 'Forgive me?'

'Anything...' Every inch of her body leaping in wild response, she found his mouth and kissed it. Hard. 'I don't want us to fight,' she breathed raggedly. 'Not us, not ever.' And she fell apart, as she always did, when he caressed her cheekbones with his large, gentle hands. Slowly, and erotically, he eased her lips apart, sliding his tongue into the moist and receptive softness of her mouth, making her want him, hotly, hungrily. Her hands flew to his shirt buttons, dragging them apart, glorying in the heated hardness of his arousal as it thrust against the softness of her tummy. But...

'Livvy, no. Not now.' His voice shook but his hands were rock-steady and just as implacable as he took hers and eased them away, stepping back, putting distance between them, an empty distance that made her ache. 'We have to work out what to do.'

Do? Her pulses were beating erratically and she couldn't think straight. It took his, 'About the low-life back there. From what he said I gathered he's related to your boss. We'll sue. No one bad-mouths my wife and gets away with it...' to bring her mind back on track.

She gave him a small, wobbly smile, pushing her tumbled hair back from her face. 'There were plenty of witnesses,' she granted, dropping gracefully onto a chintzy sofa. 'You could go ahead and sue for slander, if you think it's worth the trouble.'

'Trouble!' he repeated from behind her, his voice tight. 'He calls my wife a—'

'I know what he said,' she put in quickly. Her face was white with strain. She couldn't bear to have him pick over it. The guilt was too much to live with. She couldn't bear it if it started haunting her dreams again, doing its utmost to impinge on every aspect of her waking life, coming between them and, inevitably, sullying what she and Nathan had together.

Hurriedly pulling herself together, she stated with a calmness she was far from feeling, 'Hugh Caldwell has a vicious streak, a foul tongue. No one takes anything he says seriously.' Not even when there's a grain of truth in the murky mess? The unwelcome thought came unbidden and she thrust it aside, saying quickly, 'Which is why he has no friends, simply a few dubious acquaintances who sponge off him.' Then she added, quirkily, trying to take some of the weight out of the atmosphere, 'I gather he was a terrible disappointment to his parents.'

Deep silence. And then she heard the clink of glasses. He walked round, handed her a small whisky, took his own and dropped down onto the end of the sofa, angled into the corner, facing her, his clever eyes intent. He leaned forward, his hands between his spread knees, his glass held loosely in one hand.

'Tell me about him. He's your boss's brother? He works for the company?'

'If you could call what he does work.' She tried to answer lightly, even though she felt she had been tied down in the witness-box, that every word she said would be carefully measured and weighed.

But at least she was on marginally safer ground now that his immediate attention had been deflected away from court action whereby, even though the lies would be refuted, the grain of truth would be revealed, painting her guilty as sin.

'His job title is sales director, but his job actually appears to consist of long, boozy lunches with anyone angling for a free meal.' She took a small sip from her glass, grateful for the warmth, the tiny measure of Dutch courage. She needed it. Hugh Caldwell's vicious tongue was not going to spoil everything for her. She wouldn't let it!

'And your boss—his brother, right?—puts up with it?' He sounded disbelieving and she couldn't blame him. He didn't know the full story.

'James. Yes, he puts up with it.' Unknowingly, her voice had softened, the strained lines of her face easing under the influence of a tiny smile.

She admired James Caldwell and would do almost anything for him. Their relationship had many levels. He had helped her when she'd been emotionally bankrupt. Her loyalty, both personal and in her capacity as his PA, was absolute.

'Why?' The question was blunt, the expression she surprised at the back of his brooding eyes smacked of aggression, and something else. Suspicion. Olivia sighed wretchedly and set her glass aside.

'Family duty, perhaps. Who's to tell?' She shrugged her slim shoulders, knowing that whatever she said about James Caldwell would only fuel the embers of the argument they'd had much earlier. After hearing that wretched man's evil gossip, Nathan's desire to see her quit her job would be set in stone.

'Hugh is six years younger than James and he's always resented James for being the first-born, the brainy, good-looking son. Add to that the fact that James took over the reins of Caldwell Engineering when their father had a massive stroke ten years ago and pulled it from the bottom of the league to the top. Plus, when James's godfather died he left him a huge private fortune. Mix that lot up with a hefty dose of sexual jealousy—Hugh took a girlfriend home and she and James promptly fell in love and married six months later—and you have a recipe for resentment and spite.'

'So because he's the underdog in the Caldwell set-up, a loser, he spread malicious lies about his brother,' Nathan said, his astute eyes pinning her down. 'That figures. But why involve you?'

Olivia sucked in a sharp little breath. Her skin was burning beneath the cool white fabric of her dress. She would have given anything if they could have put the clock back, decided to stay home tonight, as she told him quietly, 'Just before I was promoted to James's PA, Hugh made a heavy pass. I was married—Max was still alive—but that didn't make any difference, not to him! Needless to say, I told him where he could go. He's probably hated me ever since.'

She tried to make it sound like nothing much, because if Nathan knew what had really happened he wouldn't rest until he'd exacted every last scrap of retribution.

But even though she'd tried to make light of the revolting incident, to pretend it hadn't been important, Nathan slapped his untouched glass down on the coffee-table and jerked to his feet. After pacing the room, he swung round to face her at last.

'So that excuses everything, does it?' he demanded. 'Just because he habitually loses out we must all turn a blind eye to the vicious lies he spreads all over the place.' There was no warmth in his eyes, his rawly sensual mouth pulled back against his teeth with grinding frustration. 'You don't have to put it into words. I can read your every thought. So confirm it for me, Livvy—you don't want to take this any further. Right?'

Her violet eyes were dark compared with the pallor of her face. She met him head-on. 'I don't see the point. As long as you don't believe his lies, I simply don't see the point. He's an unimportant, vindictive little man and no one with an ounce of sense takes him seriously.' She stood up, weariness washing through her, making her sway. 'I'll talk to James about it on Monday. Ask his opinion.'

And she felt her breath make a solid, painful lump in her throat as he lashed back, 'At the same time you hand in your resignation? Why should his opinion be more important than mine?'

Love him to pieces she certainly did, but that didn't mean she could excuse unfairness. The question of her resignation was far from settled, and he knew it. It was what their first fight had been about; did he think she'd forgotten?

But now wasn't the time to re-introduce that contentious subject so she simply pointed out, 'Ordinarily, of course not. But he is involved. And there's his wife to consider. I think they should be consulted before you start shouting for litigation, don't you?' She raked a hand through her hair, sick of the subject. 'I'm tired; I'm going to bed.'

And, for the first time in their wildly passionate relationship, he didn't follow, just watched the unknowingly sexy sway of her body with hard, assessing eyes.

Olivia, lying awake in the soft, king-sized bed some twenty minutes later, wondered desperately if things would ever be the same between them again, or if Hugh's vile tongue had sown the seeds of suspicion, seeds that would grow and spread, smothering all that had been so bright and beautiful between them, turning all that consuming passion to dust.

CHAPTER TWO

PERHAPS she had overreacted, Olivia thought, looking up with the new-day optimism that had helped her survive the bad years with Max.

And then she remembered and her heart dropped nauseatingly. Nathan hadn't joined her until the early hours, slipping between the sheets beside her, keeping woodenly to his side of the king-sized bed, being very careful not to touch her.

He was punishing her for what Hugh had said in his drunken spite, as if he'd believed every damaging word. His lack of trust appalled her. What chance did their marriage have if he became a stranger at the first stroke of trouble? No, worse than a stranger—an enemy!

Not knowing which emotion took precedence, the anger over his insulting lack of trust or the gut-wrenching misery, she squirmed up against the pillows. She saw him standing at the foot of the bed, his tanned, fantastic body gilded by the June sunlight that streamed through the open window, vigorously rubbing his wet, dark hair with a crisp white towel, making it stand up in endearing spikes.

Despite her savagely raging emotions, her body jerked in immediate wild response. He was so gorgeous; he was everything her body, her heart and soul craved. She couldn't drag her eyes away. Her skin burned beneath the lazy, sexy scrutiny of his eyes.

He dropped the towel slowly and came to the side of the bed. Her breath thickened in her throat. Six feet three inches of daunting male perfection, lean, hard and perfectly proportioned. He had the brand of graceful strength that made her mouth go dry.

Hunkering down, his warm grey eyes level with hers, he took her hands, his fingers relaxed.

'Forget last night happened. You were right—I shouldn't have taken the louse so seriously.' The pressure of his fingers increased just fractionally. 'I won't pretend I understand why you're apparently reluctant to slap the guy down in public, why you don't want to fight—but I promise you I'm trying.'

Olivia gritted her teeth, dropping her eyes. This was difficult. He was as good as accusing her of being a wimp, of having no fight in her. It was miles away from the truth. She'd been fighting all her life and wasn't about to lie down and let things happen to her now.

But, in spite of what he'd said last night, he couldn't read her mind, so he wasn't to know how hard she was fighting, fighting to keep her secret guilt away from him, keep it safely shut up inside herself where it could be ignored.

There was no answer to give to that statement, no answer she wanted to give, except, 'What's to forget? I don't remember a thing!' Her violet eyes sparkled as she drew their twined hands towards her so that the back of his fingers grazed her breasts, heard the sharp hiss of his indrawn breath as she invited rawly, 'Kiss me.'

The flash of desire deep in his eyes was unmissable and her lush mouth softened, the core of her body aching with heat, needing his lovemaking to blot out the ugly scenes of the night before, but he took a deep breath, his impressive shoulders straightening as he stood upright, releasing her clinging hands.

'Normally that's an invitation I'd find impossible to refuse,' he said. He turned, reaching for his robe, thrusting his long arms into the sleeves, tying the belt round his taut waist. 'But we both know what it would lead to, don't we? We wouldn't leave the bedroom for the rest of the day, and I already phoned Rye House before I showered. We're spending the weekend there; my parents are looking forward to seeing us.'

He was already pulling casual jeans and shirts from the dressing chest, tossing them, man-like, any old how over the back of a chair. 'We both need some breathing space and at least we won't fight in front of an audience. So pack our gear after you've showered, would you? I'll make breakfast.'

Hauling herself out of bed, Olivia felt as if her heart had been dumped about six inches beneath her feet, hating the edge she'd detected in his voice.

Not that she didn't want to visit his parents; she had taken to them immediately, relieved by their warm welcome because she'd been worried that they might think a widow, from a very ordinary background, was no great catch for their brilliant only son.

And she'd only met them twice before. The first

time when Nathan had whisked her to Bedfordshire to announce their almost immediate wedding plans to his commendably phlegmatic parents and the second time at the marriage ceremony itself. So it made perfect sense that, after a week back in England, Nathan would want to visit them. Despite his nomadic lifestyle he and his parents were very close. She might have envied him that, had not Angela and Edward welcomed her as part of the family.

But she couldn't help feeling that she and Nathan should have taken the opportunity this weekend to talk over the events of last night, get them in perspective and then, and only then, put them behind them.

But, strangely, Nathan seemed intent on sweeping it all under the carpet, forgetting everything, at least for the moment. Why? He was the most direct person she had ever encountered. Was it because he couldn't bring himself to even think about the accusations Hugh had made in case he found himself believing them?

Her eyes were clouded, her whole body tense as she towelled herself dry after her shower and walked through to the bedroom to dress and pack. Then the appetising aromas of grilling bacon and fresh, strong coffee wafted up the stairs, making her nose twitch.

It had always astounded her that a man as wealthy as Nathan Monroe, a man who could press buttons and have servants coming out of the woodwork to attend to his every need if he so wished, should know his way around a kitchen like a veteran.

Relaxing a little, she pulled on a pair of soft, well-

worn white jeans, topping them with a pansy-purple
T-shirt that reflected the colour of her eyes, and told
herself she couldn't spend the entire weekend worrying about his motives.

Besides, Rye House was quite wonderful. Set in
acres of rolling, wooded countryside, it had been in
the Monroe family since the year dot. She would, she
vowed, enjoy the weekend.

And so she did. As they were changing for dinner
that evening in the luxurious guest suite, decorated in
shades of soft old rose and misty grey, the perfect foil
for the handsome antiques that had been handed down
from generation to generation, Nathan asked, 'Glad
we came?' He was standing at the foot of the four-
poster bed, watching her mirror-image as she brushed
her long black hair. Her answering smile was warm
and genuine.

'Very.' She put her brush down, wondering if he
had any idea how sensational he looked; his soft dark
hair falling over his brow, his hands casually thrust
into the pockets of the black trousers that clipped his
long legs and sexily narrow hips, the stark white shirt
making his tan fantastic.

She lowered her eyes. Now was not the time to
entertain lustful thoughts about her husband! There
was dinner to get through and—

God, would she ever get used to the way he made
her feel? She hoped not! Getting her mind back on
track, she asked, 'Where were you all afternoon? I
missed you.'

He and Edward, his father, had disappeared directly
after lunch while she and his mother had been clearing

up, because Hilda, their daily, didn't work at weekends. And she had missed him, fretted over whether
he was deliberately avoiding her, giving himself a
slice of the space he'd said they both needed.

'Sorry about that.' She caught his cool glance in
the mirror. 'The old man's building a kit-car in the
empty stables. I told him he was in his second childhood, but when he showed me what he was doing I
was hooked. A Cobra replica body married to the
Rover V8 engine. It's going to be really something
when it's finished.'

'Toys for the boys!' She rolled her eyes in mock
exasperation. 'Why do men never grow up?'

She was trying to make a joke of it, lighten the
atmosphere, nudge them towards the old, wonderful
closeness, but he simply shrugged, walking slowly
over the polished oak boards to stand behind her.

'I can think of a few grown-up things I'd like to
do right now.' His voice was heavy as his eyes made
a slow and sultry assessment of her mirror-image,
stripping away the soft, garnet-coloured silk of her
discreetly styled, sleeveless dress.

'You are unforgivably beautiful,' he said rawly. 'I
can't look at you without wanting to take you to bed.
But you know me.' His mouth curved without humour. 'I like to get my priorities right. Is it too much
to hope that you spent the afternoon mentally com-
posing your letter of resignation?'

'I'm afraid it is,' she answered tightly, meeting his
cool eyes in the mirror, refusing to let him stare her
down. 'I won't be forced into a snap decision.' Max
had always tried to do that to her, tried to make her

fall in with his plans, using the threat of violence if she didn't. But she had stood her ground then, and would do so now. 'We need to have a proper discussion. All we've done so far is snipe at each other.'

'I see.' He sounded almost bored and turned, strolling to one of the mullioned windows to look out. 'So what's to discuss?'

Olivia bit her lip, tension making her shiver. Because her love for him was so deep it would be too easy to give in, do exactly what he wanted, but she had to stay calm, in control—she had learned that much when she'd been married to Max. If she showed any weakness he would pounce, bend her so easily to his will.

'What I want, for starters,' she said collectedly. 'But there's no time to go into all of that right now. Your mother's invited some friends to meet us—well, me, I suppose.' She searched her brain for names. 'Ruth and Lester Spencer. We'll be expected to show our faces any time now.'

He moved away from the window, taking his elegantly cut dinner jacket from the wardrobe where she'd hung it earlier. 'Then we'd better change the subject, hadn't we?' He was coolly dismissive. 'So tell me, what did you and Ma find to do with yourselves?' he tossed at her, settling the jacket snugly over his shoulders.

'Plenty.' She applied her make-up hurriedly, her hands shaking. She was still deeply affected by the undercurrent of antagonism. 'I helped her prepare the salads for the meal this evening, then she made some lemonade and we carried it out to the rose garden and simply sat and nattered.'

'What about? Were you bored out of your socks?' He was sharing the mirror, talking like a polite stranger, tying his bow-tie with expert fingers. 'Once she starts on the subject of her charity work she sends everyone to sleep. But don't tell her I told you so; the poor love would be shattered.'

'We mostly talked about you.' She capped her lipstick, her voice deliberately matching the coolness of his. 'But don't worry, I managed not to yawn.'

She watched his eyes glitter at her and wasn't going to tell him that the conversation had revealed how ignorant his doting parents were of his true desires and needs, and said instead, 'I wonder if you appreciate how lucky you are? Oh, not all this—' She gestured vaguely around the room at the lovely antique furnishings, the porcelain bowls of garden flowers set on almost every available polished surface. 'But the feeling of love and warmth that comes entirely from your parents. They obviously dote on each other and on you. Which is nice, because it rubs off on me, too. They have the happy knack of making me feel I'm at last part of a family.'

She had already told him that her parents had split up when she was five, that the modest terraced house had been sold after the divorce, she and her mother moving to a one-bedroom flat. But he had more or less accused her of keeping secrets, of telling him little or nothing about herself. So now, as she tipped her head to fix her gold stud earrings, she elaborated.

'Before Dad left us, my enduring memory is of

them fighting. I never saw him again. He hadn't wanted children; Mum never stopped telling me that. Then, oh, years later, she met a former mutual friend who told her Dad had remarried, had had three children and was completely content. It made her even more bitter. She'd told me so often that Dad had left because I was a burden he didn't want. Having to face up to the fact that he was perfectly happy with a full-blown family took the blame for the break-up from me and put it on her. After that she became impossible to live with.'

She stood up, smoothing the silky fabric of her dress over her hips, and Nathan asked slowly, 'Is that why you married so young? To get away from home?'

'Probably. Although I'd been living on my own for twelve months when I met Max,' she said dismissively. She didn't want to talk about it. But she caught his disappointment; it blanked the life from his expressive eyes.

She sucked her lower lip between her teeth, knowing intuitively that he'd wanted to hear her affirm it, tell him that her marriage to Max hadn't been born of the kind of passion they shared but had been her way out of an intolerable home situation.

But it was too late now to repair the damage and her years with Max were something she never talked about, something she never thought about if she could help it.

She glanced at her watch. 'It's time we went down. We don't want to keep dinner waiting any longer.'

The Spencers, Nathan's parents' oldest friends, were a comfortable couple, and the panelled dining room, with the tall French windows open to the soft summer evening, the oval mahogany table set with glittering crystal and the heavy family silver, was the perfect setting for convivial conversation over the hot lobster bisque and cold pheasant and salads.

More at ease after two glasses of superb wine, Olivia caught the gleaming humour in Nathan's eyes across the candlelit table and smiled at him softly, her heart lifting because she felt close to him again, knowing what he was thinking.

Angela Monroe was enthusiastically relating the success of her favourite charity work, but Olivia couldn't see anyone yawning yet and her smile deepened.

She already felt at home here, accepted, and the misery, the plain nastiness of what had happened last night had assumed the mantle of a bad dream, no more, a fading dream that would soon be entirely lost to memory.

Once he'd got over the shock of what he'd heard last night, Nathan wouldn't believe a single word of it. And sooner or later he'd agree to discuss their future, listen to what she had to say on the subject of her resignation, and they'd reach a decision they could both be comfortable with.

And she couldn't imagine, as she saw the soft glow of love in Nathan's eyes as he watched her across the table—and that couldn't be merely a trick of the candlelight, could it?—that everything could start to go wrong again. Badly wrong.

'We're really going to miss you on the committee, Ruth,' Angela sighed. 'Apart from that, I don't know what I'll do without you. If you'd asked my permission to sell up I'd have flatly refused!'

Nathan turned to Ruth Spencer, his dark brows raised in mild surprise. 'Are you and Lester moving? I thought you were as deeply rooted here as the Monroes.'

Ruth shook her head, her white curls bobbing. 'Hardly. We can't claim to have been here since William the Conqueror!' She glanced at her husband. 'We can't say it was an easy decision. But The Grange is too big for two old codgers.'

She turned to Olivia. 'Sadly, we didn't have children so we don't even have the excuse of handing the place on through the family. So we're bowing out gracefully, before we get too old to stand the trauma of moving, and retiring to the coast. We've found a manageable cottage with a small garden that's crying out for reclamation. So that leaves The Grange looking for the owners it deserves—a young family, ideally, to fill all those rooms.'

'Are you thinking what I'm thinking, Angie?' Edward grinned at his wife down the length of the table. He was still a handsome man, his iron-grey hair thick and strong, the family resemblance between him and his son unmistakable—which meant, Olivia thought contentedly, Nathan would mature spectacularly well.

'I'm sure I am!' Angela put her cutlery neatly on her plate and planted her elbows on the table, cupping her chin in her hands, her merry blue eyes fixing on Nathan's. He returned her fizzling look with an amused smile.

'Thinking of buying it, Ma? Housing a few more

homeless families? Or are we into craft centres for
struggling artisans? Whatever, I'm with you, as always. You can count on my donation.'

Watching him swallow the last of his wine, Olivia
thought she had never loved him more. The close
family bonds were evident, his interest in what his
parents were doing, his open-handed support for his
mother's charities, totally endearing. She closed her
eyes briefly, her happiness almost uncontainable.
What had she ever done to deserve Nathan's love?
She had never felt so protected, so secure, in the
whole of her life.

'No, darling, not this time.' Angela tipped her head
on one side. Her rich auburn hair had only a few
strands of silver and it glowed warmly in the subdued,
intimate lighting. 'Livvy and I had a real heart-to-
heart this afternoon. You're married now, so it's time
you put down roots and stopped jetting all over the
world like a demented gnat!' Her loving smile took
any sting out of the words, but Nathan, Olivia noted,
didn't return it. His face had closed up and her heart
sank.

'I know you have the mews cottage, which is fine,
I suppose. Livvy says she loves it, and she does have
her job to keep her occupied while you're flitting off
here and there, so for the time being I can see you
need a London base—and that's an improvement on
hotel rooms and suitcases!

'But you need somewhere bigger,' she burbled on
in blithe innocence, blissfully unaware of the building
tension. 'The Grange would be perfect. You could
come down most weekends and when the children

begin to arrive—and I hope that won't be too far
down the road—you could move in permanently. You
could fill one of the rooms with all that electronic
gadgetry people like you seem unable to function
without, and I could have my new daughter, and my
grandchildren, practically on the doorstep. I know
you'll have Rye House one day—' she crossed her
fingers elaborately and wagged them at her husband
'—but that won't be for ages yet! And it would be
lovely to have you settle so near!'

'Brilliant!'

'A splendid idea!' the Spencers enthused as one.

'You've really excelled yourself this time, Ma,'
Nathan said tonelessly. 'Take your oar out, for God's
sake! Olivia and I are more than capable of sorting
out our own future.'

Silence. Angela looked more surprised than
stricken. It was probably the first time her adored son
had slapped her down, Olivia thought. Whenever
she'd tried to interfere in his life before he would have
given her that lazy, stupendous smile and just got on
with doing exactly what he wanted to do.

Nathan had no intention of settling down; she knew
that now. There hadn't been the time or the inclination
during their brief, passionate courtship to think of
their future. They had been too obsessed with each
other.

She wished, with painful intensity, that her mother-
in-law had kept her mouth shut. The relaxed persona
Nathan had been acquiring throughout the evening
had been wiped away by his mother's artless interference.

But, even though she was shocked by his cold incisiveness, Angela wasn't to be deflected. She was his mother, after all, and entitled to open her mouth when no one else would dare.

'I'm sure you are, dear. But as The Grange is on the market it wouldn't do any harm if you took Livvy to see over it, would it, now? You could walk across tomorrow morning, if that's all right with Lester and Ruth.'

Whether or not it would be convenient no one would ever know, Olivia decided sinkingly as Nathan stated flatly, 'Not possible. We're leaving directly after breakfast. Ten, at the latest.'

It was the first Olivia had heard of it. They'd planned to spend the whole weekend here, driving back to town late on Sunday evening, but there was no point in arguing about it. Nathan had made his mind up and nothing she said would change it. She recognised with an inward shudder that his dark mood had nothing to do with his mother's well-meaning interference and everything to do with her.

And although the conversation was general for the remainder of the evening she sensed the undercurrent of his anger. She was sure everyone else was unaware; not even his parents, close as they were, could tune into his moods as instinctively as she could.

And much later, almost before he'd closed the bedroom door behind them, he drawled, 'So that was what the cosy natter was all about this afternoon? The London house, handy for your job, but it would be nice to have a country place, to put down roots, tie us down.'

'It wasn't like that,' she told him levelly, not wanting to fight. Angela had done all the talking, explaining that Nathan had always had itchy feet, always off someplace else, doing deals, turning wheels. Seizing happily on the fact of his marriage as evidence that he was at long last willing to settle down. 'The idea that we should consider buying The Grange came as a complete surprise to me, too.'

She walked out of her shoes and took the studs from her ears, searching for a way to put things right between them. 'Your parents know I work—it's only natural for them to look into the future, see me giving it up when we start a family, needing somewhere bigger. Everything set out in a nice predictable line.'

She had her back to him, putting the gold studs safely in their soft silk pouch, and only knew he was right behind her when his hands fastened on her shoulders, twisting her round to face him.

'Did you tell her I'd begged you to hand in your resignation?' He forced her chin up with his fingers. 'Look at me. I want to see your eyes. I can tell if you're lying. Did you?'

'No.' She held his gaze squarely, her violet eyes bruised. The lovely guest suite suddenly seemed an alien place. She didn't want to be here. The matter of her resignation had nothing to do with anyone else. His fingers tightened on her chin, hurting her. She tried to twist away but he wouldn't let her. She hated having him touch her in anger. It brought back sickening memories of Max.

'Why not? Because you have no intention of doing what I asked?' His voice was low, deadly. 'The whole world is my workplace; you knew that before we married. You're my wife; I want you with me. But you don't see it that way—'

'My career's important too,' she retorted, her teeth snapping. Why did men always think they and their needs were the most important things in a relationship? Why should women always be the ones who had to adapt?

'I offered you another, remember? Helping me. Taking the place of the temps I hire in wherever I happen to be. What makes the job at Caldwell's more exciting and challenging than that? More satisfying than being with me?' He released her, his hands dropping to his sides. 'If you loved me, you'd want to be with me,' he said flatly. 'Or was Big-Mouth telling the truth? Can't you bear to leave James Caldwell?'

CHAPTER THREE

'THIS is getting to be a habit.' Nathan's voice came softly in the thick, curtained darkness. He turned his head towards her. 'Let's say we kick it?'

Lying a rigid three feet away, in the intimate cave of the unfamiliar four-poster bed, Olivia wanted to slap him. The sultry, sexy tone of his voice told her he was perfectly happy to forget his temper, the hurtful things it had made him say. But she couldn't.

They hadn't made love for thirty-six hours so he was probably frustrated. His rampant male hormones were making him forget the way he'd accused her of refusing to walk away from her job because she was having an ongoing affair with her boss.

Well, she hadn't forgotten and if he had the nerve to reach out and touch her she would scream—even if it did bring his parents to the guest suite at a run!

She held her breath, all tensed up inside, her eyes hurting from staring into the darkness while she waited for that sneaky hand, that strong, sinfully knowing, sneaky hand, to bridge the gap and begin to work that wicked magic, taking what he wanted...

Which was exactly what she wanted, too. Her body was already responding dramatically. It would be too easy to turn into his arms, pretend that that would resolve everything. The thought appalled her. She blinked her eyes rapidly and made herself breathe. It would be so easy…

'I can't forget what you accused me of that easily,' she said, making her words clipped and precise so he wouldn't guess how much she wanted to be held in his arms, to be physically assured of his love—wild passion absorbing all their senses, blanking out the frightening knowledge that he couldn't love her at all if he didn't trust her. 'A quick grope won't make everything all right.'

'Is that what you think of our lovemaking?' he came back at her immediately, his voice as cold and bleak as outer space. 'A quick grope?'

Too late, Olivia wished she'd held her stupid, wilful tongue, done the dignified thing and simply exited the bed, walked out with her head in the air to make herself a nice cup of tea in Angela's kitchen, as any sane woman would have done in the circumstances. Or looked for Edward's brandy and poured herself an enormous dose, which was probably a much better idea…

Instead it was Nathan who swung out of bed, reached for his robe. She couldn't see him but could hear his impatient movements. She wriggled up on one elbow, the fear that he was cutting himself off from her, somehow moving away from her, never, truly, to return—not in spirit, anyway—making her voice sharp.

'Where are you going?' If he mentioned tea or brandy, or even her most hated all of panaceas—cocoa—she would join him. Yes, she would, she decided, getting ready to scramble out of bed.

She sagged dejectedly back against the pillows when he drawled at her, 'To make a couple of phone calls. You have the bed to yourself to sulk in. And don't worry, wife of my heart, I won't creep back for a furtive grope.'

Oh, what had made her say that? she thought with anguish as the door closed behind him with a quiet control that told her he'd gone far beyond mere anger.

Tears welled up and ran down her cheeks, slow and fat and born of self-disgust. She hated herself! Of course she didn't equate the magic of their lovemaking with a quick grope—surely he knew that? Couldn't he understand that she'd been getting her own back for what he had said earlier?

Flicking on the bedside light, she reached for a handful of tissues, blew her nose and scrubbed her wet cheeks. She had to put things right. Make him understand that she hadn't meant what she'd said, that she hadn't been rejecting him but the accusations he'd made.

It was more than time to find out if he really, or even partially, believed the things Hugh had said. They couldn't get on with their future while he kept a question mark in his mind.

The satin of her robe was cold against her heated skin. She shivered, tying the sash around her waist, sudden indecision making her frown.

He was making a couple of phone calls, he'd said, so right now wouldn't be the best time to attempt a reconciliation, would it? And at this time of night that could only mean he was contacting somewhere halfway round the world.

But that didn't mean he was so annoyed with her he was planning on taking the next available flight out to wherever, did it?

The attempted reassurance didn't work. She chewed on the corner of her lip and her legs began to shake. She sank back on the edge of the bed. She knew enough about his business life to admire the way he'd made himself an enviable fortune, travelling the world looking for investment opportunities, playing the stock market, building stakes in groups to sell on at a profit.

It would be possible, he'd once told her, to conduct most of his business from a well-equipped office, but he preferred the hands-on approach. Was he planning one of his extended foreign business trips to punish her?

Speculation was getting her nowhere. And he wouldn't be on the phone all night. She crawled back into bed and propped herself up against the pillows, waiting for him.

As soon as he showed his face she'd make everything right between them again, she promised herself. Yes, she most definitely would. And it wouldn't be too long now, just long enough for him to make those calls. She'd give him that much space; she owed him that. He wouldn't stay away for the rest of the night.

But he had. Still in her robe, propped against the pillows, disorientated because she wasn't in her own, familiar surroundings, Olivia woke from fretful dreams, deeply annoyed with herself. She had gone

and fallen asleep before he'd come back to bed, and
nothing had been put right.

Turning to remedy the unthinkable situation, her
body tensed up. His side of the bed was well and truly
empty. Had her seeming rejection, her refusal to behave as if nothing had happened, angered him to the
point of refusing to be anywhere near her? She felt
physically sick.

They met on the sweeping staircase, that much admired feature of Rye House. But she wasn't up to
admiring the Grinling Gibbons carvings right now.
She'd showered and dressed quickly, intent on routing
him out, dreading the possibility of discovering that
their beautiful relationship had been damaged, vowing
that she wouldn't let it be.

'Where were you?' she demanded, refusing to
flinch beneath those cold grey eyes. He was fully
dressed and looked as if he hadn't slept at all.

'Working.' He stopped on his loping way up. 'I
came up to shower and dress at six. You were dead
to the world. I've been sent to fetch you down for
breakfast.'

She didn't want any. Her stomach was in knots. He
was looking at her with a stranger's eyes. It frightened
her. But she wasn't going to let it show.

'Punishing me for denting your ego, you mean,' she
retorted, resisting the impulse to shout because one or
other of his parents could put in an appearance at any
time. But she was sickened by the obvious lie. If their
marriage was to grow and flourish they had to be hon-
est with each other. She hated evasions of any kind;
she'd had enough of those from Max to last her a

dozen lifetimes. She stared straight back at him. 'Admit it. How could you possibly work? Here, in the middle of the night? You were sulking!'

'I could work on a clothes-line,' he informed her coldly. 'A telephone, paper, a pen—I don't need much more. And sulking's a woman's game, one that cuts no ice with me. Coming?'

She looked at his merciless, sensual mouth and shuddered in primitive response. Fighting it, she made her lush lips as prim as they could be. She didn't want to kiss him—no, she did not. She wanted to shake him!

Trying to smile for his parents' sake, she got herself into the kitchen by will-power alone. The smell of bacon made her feel ill.

'You mustn't let him get away with it!' Angela stated. 'Working through the night—there's no need for it! And he used most of my headed notepaper, too!' She pointedly moved a bunch of papers out of the way and put a loaded toast rack down on the huge kitchen table.

'It was all I could find; I'll get it replaced,' Nathan said with a tight smile. 'And don't nag, Ma; it makes you sound old.'

Olivia's face ached with the effort of trying to look pleasant and unconcerned, as if she were totally in tune with her new husband's odd working habits— sympathetic, even faintly amused.

Edward sauntered in, sniffing the air. 'Is breakfast nearly ready? I'm starving! It's a shame you two have to rush off this morning. You could have helped me with the Cobra—' He broke off as he caught his wife's withering look and amended, 'Or gone to church with your mother. We'd planned on lunching at the golf club. They put on a passably good roast. No eggs for me, Angie.' His youthful eyes smiled into Olivia's. 'When I remember, I try to watch my cholesterol intake. Pour the coffee, would you, Livvy? I'm gasping. Are you sure you won't change your minds and stay?'

Pouring coffee into the wide-bowled cups, Olivia left Nathan to convince his parents that they had to make tracks.

'There are several things I need to sort out,' he answered tersely as his mother set a huge plate of bacon and eggs in the centre of the table.

'Help yourselves,' she invited. 'Do you know how forbidding you sound, Nat? ''Things to sort out'', indeed.' She took her place and shook out her napkin. 'You need never do another stroke. You could retire tomorrow, and you know it. Workaholics don't make the best husbands, isn't that right, Livvy?'

'I'm working on it!' Which probably hadn't been the most tactful thing to say, she decided, feeling those cold grey eyes on her, boring right through her. But she did her best to look cheerful, eating hardly anything while trying to look as if she was enjoying every mouthful—just waiting for the time when she and Nathan could be alone to sort out the uncomfortable mess they'd somehow got themselves into.

But being alone didn't necessarily mean being closer, she discovered as they drove away from Rye House not long after breakfast. The silence was grim.

Her heart lurching, she broke it. 'I'm sorry about

last night. You must know I didn't mean it.' She
flicked him a hopeful sideways look but his profile
was stony. Swallowing a ragged sigh, trying not to
plead, she offered, 'Listen, we have to discuss it ra-
tionally—everything. Hugh, James, my job, even
Angie's bright idea about buying that house. Everything.'

They had left the tangle of narrow country lanes
behind and Nathan put his foot down. The big car
responded throatily and Olivia's stomach jumped up
into her mouth. She just hoped there weren't any
speed cameras about. She said thickly, 'I hate this
atmosphere. I don't know about you, but I want things
back the way they were. We love each other,' she
stated desperately. 'It should be simple enough!'

'It is simple enough.' His voice was as smooth and
precise as his driving style. 'You know what I want.
When you've reached a decision, tell me. Until then
there's little we can usefully discuss. Think about it.'

Oh, yes, she knew what he wanted. She closed her
eyes wearily. Each time her resignation had come up
for discussion he'd grown more insistent.

It had started off fairly innocuously, Nathan rea-
sonably pointing out that she didn't need to work, that
her job would keep them apart, that he wanted her
with him wherever he went. Desperately torn, she had
tried to explain that she would have to think about it.

'James threw a fit when I told him we were getting
married and asked for two months' honeymoon
leave,' she'd told him. 'But he gave in and said,
"Anything, so long as I know the best PA I'm ever
likely to get isn't walking out permanently."' She'd

smiled then, confident that he loved her enough to understand that she couldn't simply phone through, as he appeared to expect her to, and say she wasn't coming back. 'I guess I'd have to train someone else up, and that could take time.'

But Nathan hadn't seen it that way. 'He doesn't own you,' he'd said. Implying that he did, Olivia had thought, beginning to bristle, appalled by the first coldness she'd seen in his eyes. And it had been then that he'd broken the uncomfortable tension between them, suggesting a restaurant and nightclub. And after that, after overhearing Hugh's scandalous remarks, he'd stopped trying gentle persuasion and was now insisting.

He had, she recognised hollowly, issued an ultimatum. And told her to think about it.

She didn't want to.

She loved him to distraction. She would willingly die for him. But he had to see that she wasn't going to let herself be bullied into doing something she knew would make her uncomfortable with herself. Max had done that too many times; she wouldn't allow it to happen again.

Yet the prospect of deepening the rift between them by refusing to do meekly exactly as he said, exactly when he said it heaped her heart with deep misery.

She twisted her hands in her lap, her fingers sliding over the engagement ring he'd given her, sliding and stroking it as if that would bring back the gloriously happy recent past. An amethyst in an ornate, heavy gold setting.

'To match the colour of your eyes,' he'd told her,

slipping it onto her finger, his eyes dark and liquid with love.

She remembered that day so vividly, and the days that had gone before, the days that had come after. She would never forget a single second, and clung to the comfort of her shining memories, remembering how they'd met.

It had been a cold spring day and she'd been sure that sudden, heavy rain showers had been programmed to put in an appearance at a time calculated to cause as much nuisance to herself, personally, as possible.

She'd dropped by the local supermarket on her way home from work and was heading down the street, blinded by rain, carrying the makings of her supper in the flimsy supermarket carrier bag, the thin plastic digging into her fingers.

And the bag had split, tipping her purchases onto the streaming pavement. Cursing under her breath, she'd bent to retrieve what was salvageable, growling with disbelief as a well-polished, handmade shoe stomped on her slices of cold ham. Bouncing up, she'd collided with a lean, male body, felt his steadying hands on her shoulders, and lifted her head to glare at him. And that was when it had happened.

'I wasn't looking where I was going.' His grey eyes held hers with the dawning of delight. It was as if, she thought, he recognised her from a long way back, was welcoming her wholeheartedly into his life again.

They had never met before, she knew that; of course she did. But she felt she had known him all her life, had been waiting for him.

The rain came down as if it were trying to flood them out of existence and they simply stood there, oblivious to the torrents, aware only of each other. So shatteringly aware.

And in that timeless moment she lost every scrap of common sense she'd ever had, forgot the solemn promises she'd made to herself about never being stupid enough to fall in love again—because it had happened, and she was soaringly, ecstatically glad.

'We'll drown!' His sudden, spectacular grin shook her to pieces. One hand slid down to take hers. Her fingers curled around his and the sensation of his warm skin on hers was unbelievable. It made her whole body come alive, made her feel that until this moment she'd been half dead and hadn't realised it.

With his free hand he retrieved her scattered supper, dumping the sodden mess into a litter bin. Then, his fingers entwined possessively in hers, he tugged her over to his waiting car.

Long, low, gun-metal grey, it looked dangerous. And that suited her, she thought, allowing herself to be gently tucked into the passenger seat. She felt wild, her blood hot, coursing wickedly through her veins.

'Where are you taking me?' She didn't stop to ask herself if getting into a car with a strange male was the wisest move she had ever made. She was soaked to the skin, her suit ruined, the weight of the rain water dragging her luxuriant hair from its workaday moorings. She knew she looked a mess and couldn't stop smiling.

'My hotel.' She noted the smile tugging at his mouth, too, as he eased the car out into the flow of traffic. 'You can dry out while I feed you. It's the least I can do after ruining your groceries.'

The feeling of belonging, truly belonging to someone swamped her. It was a mystery she couldn't explain, an inevitable happening. She asked, 'Are you married?'

'No. Are you?'

'I was. He died three years ago.'

He gave her a swift, intense look, his dark brows drawn together. Then he turned his attention back to the road—or at least what he could see of it through the driving rain, the wipers barely coping. 'And now?'

'There's been no one since. I'm married to my career.'

His wickedly gorgeous mouth curved. 'That I can cope with; a career's no competition.'

'What are you competing for?' How strange, she thought, her eyes bright with silent laughter, to be sitting here, having this conversation. She didn't even know his name.

'The right to have you in my bed.' Softly spoken, musing, almost, his reply took her breath away.

By any standards she should be demanding he stop, let her out. But she didn't. She didn't even ask him if he thought she was the type of woman who would go to bed with a man, any man, any time. She knew, with a deep instinctive joy, that he didn't think any such thing.

She simply asked, 'When do you see that happening?' knowing what his answer would be before he gave it.

'When you're ready. When you understand, as I did

the moment I looked into your eyes, that we're two halves of a whole.'

Tangled black lashes veiled her eyes as she slumped weakly back in her seat, her arms hugging her body as she tried to contain the happiness that transcended anything she had experienced before. She felt weak with it, and could hardly stand when he exited the now stationary vehicle and walked round to hand her out.

They were in front of the city's most luxurious hotel and she leant into the support of his possessive arm, blinking the rain out of her eyes, as a liveried doorman hurried towards them with an umbrella, another taking the car keys to park the sleek grey monster.

'Dreadful day, Mr Monroe.' Sheltering beneath the huge umbrella, they were deferentially escorted up the wide stone steps.

So his name was Monroe. She smiled to herself, a wriggle of happiness further weakening her knees as she heard him correct, 'You're wrong there, Ben, old son. It's the most perfect day that ever dawned!' His arm tightened around her tiny waist and she was too dazed to take in her surroundings, leaning against him as the lift took them to the top of the building, feeling utterly, blissfully secure, the warmth of it lapping over her, binding her completely.

His suite was a quiet statement of restrained elegance, not sumptuous or overpowering but an essay in refined simplicity, and her eyes went wide, taking it in. It would cost a fortune to stay here. The atmosphere was so rarefied, she felt the first stirrings of misgiving.

'You're shivering.' He took her pale hands, warming them between his, but she corrected him.

'I honestly hadn't noticed.' Her eyes swept the room expressively. 'Coming face to face with how the other half lives shook me, I guess.'

'You'll get used to it.' If his smile warmed her, his eyes scorched her. She felt herself melting away, clinging to the reality of his hands, the strong bones and warm skin reassuring, letting her know this wasn't merely a fabulous dream, that she wouldn't wake and find herself alone. 'When I need to be in London I stay here. I tend to live out of suitcases. I could function almost as well from a decently equipped office, with a couple of dedicated permanent staff, but I prefer to be where the action is, hiring secretaries, translators where necessary.' He had knelt, removing her sodden shoes, and now stood again to unbutton her jacket.

'But what we both do to earn a crust isn't important.' His eyes were soft, smiling, his voice a low, beguiling seduction in itself. 'Tell me your name.'

That made her smile—the absurdity of the way they were so close, belonged together, yet still didn't know anything practical. 'Olivia.'

'It suits you. Nathan Monroe,' he supplied. 'So tell me about yourself.' He helped her out of her jacket, the soaked fabric clinging to the silk of her blouse. 'For starters, what are your favourite foods.'

She laughed aloud at that. 'Oh, it's got to be genuine Italian ice cream.' He was leading her through to the bathroom, which was pale blue and cream marble with a half-sunken bath that looked big enough to swim in. 'And English fish and chips, of course, wrapped in newspaper with plenty of salt and vinegar—that's got to be near the top of the list!'

'It surely doesn't show.'

His eyes glinted approval as they comprehensively swept the length of her trim body and she answered breathlessly, something inside her coming to boiling point, 'I don't allow myself to indulge too often. You can have too much of a good thing.'

'I'd have to disagree with that.' His slow, beautiful smile stunned her and again his eloquent eyes made their explicit discovery, and everywhere they touched, all her secret places, her body turned to flame, aching for him, trembling for him, burning...

She had never experienced anything so erotic in her life and the way he turned and began to fill the bath only added to the tension, the pressing, urgent tension of knowing they had embarked on a journey that could have only one possible ending.

She wrapped her arms about her unbearably sensitised body, watching him. He had already discarded his jacket and the fine white fabric of his shirt accentuated those wide shoulders and the subtle play of muscle and bone as he tested the temperature of the water, added bath-oil, creating a cloud of exotically perfumed steam.

Weak with desire, she only realised she'd been holding her breath when he straightened, turning to her and loosening his tie as he said, 'Hop in. Have a good soak to chase away the chill.' He was already at the door. 'Put your wet things out; I'll see they're laundered.'

And as the door closed behind him a different and deeper type of joy engulfed her. Had he chosen to join her in the bath she would have been unable to do a single thing about it. That he hadn't, that he was willing to wait, reinforced that utterly priceless commodity: trust.

Warm, dry and wrapped in the soft terry robe he'd left draped over a gilded chair for her, Olivia ventured out into the main living area, her bare feet sinking in inches of softly luxurious pile.

Her soft, lush mouth was quivering slightly, her pansy-coloured eyes wide as uncertainty snagged the breath in her throat. For the first time since their meeting she felt unsure of herself, felt like a foolish young girl again, her woman's body swamped by pale blue towelling, her face scrubbed clean, her long hair hanging damply down her back.

Could it really have happened? Something had happened, that was for sure. Happened to her. She had fallen instantly in love with Nathan Monroe—but how could he possibly feel the same way?

'Livvy.' He rose from a soft leather armchair and his smile, the look in his eyes as he held out his hands to her banished the doubts as swiftly and efficiently as the heat of the sun dissolved morning mists.

He had changed into well-worn denims and a black cotton sweater, and his feet, like hers, were bare. Taking her into his arms, he looked deeply into her eyes, held her soul with his, and then he kissed her. Kissed her so gently, with such expert care, he made her want to cry with the incandescent beauty of the moment.

She reached up to touch his face, lovingly, wonderingly, absorbing the essence of him through her fingertips, and he took them and kissed them, one by one. She felt the sudden jolt of his heart against her breasts, felt his body tense, harden, then saw through dazed eyes that slightly crooked, splintering grin as he stepped away just slightly.

'I promised to feed you, my darling.' He pressed a button near the doorway. 'And while we eat you can tell me all there is to know about you. I want every last detail.' He led her to an exquisitely set table in a far alcove and, before she'd had time to admire and wonder at the fabulously delicate china, the heavy silverware, the delicate flower arrangements, he had given her a flute of champagne and nodded his straight-faced approval as a dignified waiter padded silently through the suite bearing newspaper-wrapped parcels, his face perfectly impassive.

'The best fish and chips to be found in the whole of London, or so I'm reliably assured,' Nathan told her, and Olivia laughed aloud as she unwrapped the steaming bundle set before her on an exquisite china plate, refusing the elegant cutlery, using her fingers. Barely had she licked the last one clean than the newspaper package was almost reverently removed and a silver goblet of ice cream placed before her.

It had, she decided, closing her eyes as she savoured the first delicious spoonful, an authentic Italian pedigree, and she was floating on a pink cloud of happiness because he'd gone to so much trouble to please her, insisting that the prestigious hotel serve such a ridiculously incongruous down-market meal.

'You've told me remarkably little about yourself,' Nathan said as the waiter left them alone with the coffee. He leaned back in his chair, his eyes lazy, smiling. 'And perhaps you're right. Our future's the most important thing. It's the most important thing we have.'

She was close to tears when Nathan finally parked in front of the mews cottage. And her voice was thick as she blurted impulsively, 'Remember how we met—how it was for us? Remember you told me our future was the most important thing we had? Don't let's put it in jeopardy, Nat.' Her eyes beseeched him to turn to her, reassure her, but he stared straight ahead.

His voice was almost offhand as he told her, 'The ball's in your court. You know what you need to do.' He cut the engine and, as he left the car without so much as a glance in her direction, Olivia's world fell to pieces and she didn't know how she was going to put it together again.

CHAPTER FOUR

OLIVIA followed Nathan into the cottage. She was doing her best to keep calm. He was treating her like a pariah and it seemed set to go on and on until she knuckled under and did exactly what he wanted her to do.

She hadn't known he could be so arrogantly autocratic, but then she knew little more about the essential him than he knew about her. She had believed they knew each other instinctively, intuitively, immediately, on some deep and unbreachable level, but, obviously, they had a lot to discover about each other.

But she did know that the pattern for their future relationship was about to be set. If she allowed him to dictate to her now, allowed him to get away with a refusal to listen to her viewpoint, then he would walk all over her for the rest of their lives!

It was a fraught situation but she had to stay calm; yelling, stamping her feet, shouting the odds would get her nowhere. They had to talk the problem over, reach an acceptable compromise. Surely he could understand the need for that?

She watched him carry their weekend luggage up the stairs, her heart like lead. Everything was changing. She couldn't bear it. Even the little house was no longer welcoming—she felt like an intruder, as if she had no right to be here.

Which was pretty paranoid—not to mention down-right feeble, she decided, hurrying on up after him. He was in their bedroom, bending over the open suitcase, fishing out the papers he'd covered with his bold, slashing, handwritten notes the night before.

Taking a big deep breath, she walked calmly over, putting her fingers lightly on the tanned skin of his forearm, feeling his whole body go tense and still at her touch.

'Let's discuss this, darling.' Her tone was hopeful now, almost buoyant. The simple touch of skin on skin was enough to set them both on fire, make them so physically aware of each other that nothing else mattered. And, proving it, his cheekbones were slashed with dull colour, his eyes glittering darkly as he straightened slowly and half turned to face her.

He dragged in a sharp breath, his eyes narrowing on her parted lips, as if he was reliving in his mind every wildly passionate kiss they'd ever shared. And with a stab of elation and of complete certainty she knew they were too much in love to let something like the question of whether she should hold onto her job or not come between them.

'There's nothing to discuss,' he answered flatly, pulling his eyes away from her face as he gathered his papers. 'You know what I want. As I've already told you, it's your decision entirely.'

'I can't believe it!' She wasn't sure whether she'd spoken aloud, or just inside her head. What she was sure of, though, was her own stupidity. She hadn't taken his utterly frustrating brand of male stubbornness into account. She felt cold inside. Defeated.

He wanted her, but he wanted his own way more.

'I'll be in the study for the next couple of hours.' He walked past her. 'It should give you time to decide what to do about your job.'

Sheer, mind-bending rage that he refused to listen to anything she might want to say had her twisting round, reaching the door ahead of him. With an almighty effort, she curbed the self-defeating anger, making her voice reasonable, consciously level as she said, 'Look, let's be adult about this.'

But she could do nothing about the flood of adrenalin pumping frantically through her veins. Couldn't hide the effects, the hectic colour that suffused her creamy skin, widening her eyes, making them glitter like precious stones, her breath coming raggedly, making her breasts push against the fine, silky fabric of her top.

His eyes dropped, drawn to the clearly defined, peaked globes.

'I can be as adult as you want me to be.'

His voice had thickened. She knew what he meant, what he wanted. He'd fought it only moments ago; she'd watched him; she'd seen how clinically he'd been able to separate himself from her.

'Livvy—' He wasn't fighting now, she thought exultantly. A trembling started deep inside her. She felt powerful and yet strangely humbled by the strength of the emotions she could rouse in him.

He reached out a hand and touched her hair, and then her face, tenderly, his love for her burning through the softly exploring tips of his fingers. She adored him, loved him more than life itself, but she owed it to herself, and to him, to demand the right to be heard. To unquestioningly give in to his every demand would diminish her, make her less than the woman he had fallen in love with.

Helplessly, Olivia closed her eyes. She was drifting, her body opening sweetly, like a flower, curving into the hard, hot strength of his.

'I want you too. So much. But, Nat, we do need to talk.' With an effort, she forced her eyes to open. Her lids were heavy. She looked at him earnestly through tangled lashes, willing him to agree.

'No talk.' He roped her long hair around his wrist, pulling her closer. 'No arguments, sweetheart. Just this.' His lips took hers with sweet persuasion. 'This is the one way I know I can make you do anything,' he murmured against her lush mouth, an unforgivable trickle of humour threading through his voice.

Her hands slid into his hair, her fingers digging into his scalp as she tried to keep herself under some kind of control. Making love with him was wonderful, irresistible, an unbreakable law of nature as far as she was concerned, but they needed to talk things through, lay down a few ground rules. And, yes, she was totally malleable when he touched her, smiled that soft, sexy, shattering smile, looked at her in that special way.

'Unfair,' she protested feebly, and felt the touch of his smile on her lips and, suddenly, resentment bubbled up inside her, swift and hot, making her tug at his hair, jerk her head away.

'Smug bastard! Don't I have a say in anything?'

He looked at her long and hard, still holding her
by her glossy black hair. He wasn't smiling now.

'You want an answer?' He gave it to her, whether
she wanted one or not, his mouth possessing hers with
savage passion, his body forcing her against the door,
his breathing ragged, and, as if her response was programmed into her, preordained, she melted into him,
her wildly tugging fingers stroking now, stroking the
beautifully formed skull beneath the soft, thick hair,
her lips opening hungrily to receive his deepening
kiss.

And then, because he knew her body intimately,
knew every shade and degree of her desire, his hands
and mouth gentled, touching her, shaping, coaxing.
Her fingers slid down, beneath the hem of his T-shirt,
stroking the firm, warm skin across his taut stomach,
and she heard his shuddering, indrawn breath, felt the
tightening of his muscles beneath her hand and knew
desire was coursing through his bloodstream, thick
and sharp and heavy.

In this way they knew each other so well.

'My dear love...' he murmured softly. 'How you
please me...'

Lost, but not too lost to tease, she stroked a finger-
tip across his parted lips, then slowly lowered her
hand, moving it sensually over his gorgeous body,
loving every inch of him. Then, in slow motion, she
undid the pearly buttons down the front of her blouse,
one by tantalising one, letting it drift away from her
shoulders, watching him watching her as her slender
fingers went with a sultry lack of haste to the front-
fastening clasp of her silk and lace bra.

'Witch!' He took over the small task, his hands sure, quick, his knuckles rubbing against the heavy, rounded curves. And for a moment his eyes devoured her hotly, before he sucked in his breath and tore off his T-shirt, gathering her into his arms, their skin a fusion of ecstasy. 'In this there can be no argument, my darling.' His voice was low, his lips moving against the silky fall of her hair. 'Just you. Just me.' Then he swept her into his arms and carried her to the waiting bed.

Olivia lay in the soft bed on that soft summer afternoon, her body warm, sated, her lush mouth bearing the brand of his passion.

Languidly, one hand snaked out, stroking the space where he had been. She must have slept for a couple of hours at least. Her mouth curved in a smile. Nathan's stamina was awesome; catching up on a lost night's sleep was a luxury he would scorn.

Soon, she would shower and dress and go and rout him out of his study, the small room at the back of the house he'd had equipped with the latest electronic gadgetry, allowing him to keep pace with the world's money markets, to contact anyone, any time, any place.

She closed her eyes again. First, she had to assemble her thoughts, sift through them calmly. She owed it to them both.

Fact number one, she ticked off in her mind: until the question of quitting her job had cropped up Nathan had never shown a hint of male chauvinism. Since the day they'd met his first concern had always been for her, her well-being, comfort, pleasure always uppermost in his mind.

After her unhappy years with Max, where complete selfishness had been the norm, Nathan's consideration, his sensitive caring had been a mind-blowing revelation. He'd made her feel so secure, so pampered, so adored.

Even when they'd started to bristle at each other, when he'd told her he expected her to give up her job, the career she'd carved out for herself, he'd deliberately cooled it. She'd known then in her heart that she'd bring him round to her way of thinking, make him see that she couldn't simply walk away from a job that had meant so much to her for so many years without giving it a lot of thought. That was fact number two.

It had all changed when he'd overheard what Hugh had been saying in that nightclub.

And that was fact number three.

The poisonous seeds had been sown. And it was up to her to make sure they didn't flourish.

Jumping out of bed, she grabbed fresh clothes and went through to shower. He'd asked her if what Hugh had said had all been foul lies, and she'd felt insulted. Her own deep guilt had made her ultra-sensitive, very much on the prickly defensive.

Trying hard to see everything from his point of view, she dressed quickly in a green cotton shirt and the favourite hip-skimming white jeans, pushed her feet into cool sandals and went down to the kitchen to make a pot of tea.

She was humming lightly, slightly out of tune,

happy. She loved her kitchen. 'Country style,' she'd said when he'd asked for her preference. 'But not twee.'

'The lady's wish is law.' He'd punctuated every word with a lazily savouring kiss, uncaring of their audience, the head designer and co-ordinator of one of the most prestigious interior design companies around.

His arms warmly encircling her, he'd added, 'Law, is that understood? Whatever the lady wants, the lady gets.' His arm had dropped, his hand moulding her bottom, stroking, curving, driving her wild. And she'd known that two seconds after the designer had left Nat would be making passionate love to her on the bare boards of the as yet unfurnished house that was to be their future home.

Such a wealth of beautiful memories. They were the best and most valuable of all riches, she mused, her eyes starry. Quite without price.

She was busy with the tray of tea things when she felt his arms go around her, pulling her back against his body.

'I thought you were working.' She half turned her head, nuzzling it into the angle of his shoulder, inhaling the musky, male scent of him.

'Was.' He rested his chin on the top of her head, his long fingers splayed against her stomach. 'Then I got the brilliant idea of waking you with a tray of tea. And if you were suitably knocked out, thanked me prettily enough, I thought I'd reward you with a repeat performance. You went to sleep on me, remember?'

'Only when your attentions had exhausted us both,'

she reminded him, her voice low and husky, a purr of laughter running through it.

Already she could feel the force of his desire against the small of her back, the seductive stroke of his hands as they inched upwards towards her breasts. And again she was floating, drifting, losing herself...

Briskly, absolutely forcing herself, she plucked his hands away from her body, hating the sudden sensation of coldness that was left behind, reached out to unplug the now ferociously boiling kettle then turned to face him, her eyes serious in her suddenly pale face.

There was heady male confidence in his smile, in his eyes. He fully believed she'd broken the intimate moment simply to deal with the kettle, that she'd slip willingly back into his arms.

He was holding his hands out to her. She made herself ignore them.

She didn't want to. But for now she must.

A dark brow drifted up in amused query. 'Teasing again, Livvy? You know where that gets you, don't you?'

She shook her head, putting a finger over his lips to silence him, and that was a mistake because he caught her hand, held it, kissing the long white fingers that instinctively curled around his.

It would be so easy—too easy—to let him lead her again into their private world of passion, the exquisite place that existed for them alone, where nothing intruded, nothing mattered but their love, their deeply devouring need for each other.

But there were things that had to be said, should have been said long before now. She had allowed herself to be sidetracked before and it mustn't happen again. So she said then, her voice firm, 'This is serious. I think I know why you want me to walk out of my job—'

'To spend your time with me, your husband. I think that was the drift of my argument.' His eyes had gone flat, his voice dry. He released her hands.

Refusing to be deterred by his spiritual and physical withdrawal, she countered, 'You won't even consider a compromise. That worried me at first because I didn't understand it. I didn't believe you could be so arrogant.'

'Believe it.' His voice was cold, his eyes colder. He swung a ladder-back chair away from the chunky pine table and sat down, his long legs stretched out in front of him, his hands crossed behind his head. 'I can be as arrogant as I need to be. And if there were a viable compromise to be found I'd consider it.'

'Then consider this—' She perched on the edge of the table, her legs swinging, not allowing herself to be intimidated by his quellingly cold and haughty act. 'You do as much work as you can from the study, right here at home. You said it was possible, remember? You could even hire a permanent assistant instead of relying on your usual temps. I keep my career, and we only need to spend time apart when it's absolutely essential you travel. That way we both get what we want.'

'No.' No vehemence, simply a flat refusal. 'I won't be cooped up in a box.' He gave her a cool, derisive glance. 'Any more compromises on offer?'

Olivia blinked the hurt from her eyes. They'd only

been living in their wonderful home for a little over a week and already he was looking on it as a prison. She remembered the fun they'd had working with the designer to get everything planned before the wedding so that everything would be in place, perfect, on their return from honeymoon, and could have cried.

'If I could come up with a dozen, you wouldn't listen,' she told him levelly, not letting herself show how much his words had hurt her. 'And, basically, I don't think you're a selfish man.' She took a deep breath. 'Hugh Caldwell did the damage, didn't he? It's not my career, as such, you object to. You want me away from James. You can't help believing there might be a grain of truth in what he said.'

All the time she'd been speaking she'd been watching him closely, convinced she'd got it right, knowing that if it had been the other way round she would have had a hard time keeping niggling suspicions, wriggling worms of doubt out of her head. But even so the fury of his reaction shattered her.

He shot to his feet, a paste-white line around his mouth as he bit out tightly, 'I don't want to believe it, dammit! Prove he was lying,' he challenged. 'Walk out of the job tomorrow and bloody well prove it!'

CHAPTER FIVE   ·

THE raw emotion in Nathan's eyes flayed Olivia, the degree of his distrust making her nauseous. She twisted her lower lip between her teeth, trying not to cry.

'I shouldn't have to prove a thing. Especially not to you.' Her voice was fractured. Her lovely kitchen was swimming with sunshine but she felt cold, right through to the centre of her bones. She wrapped her arms around her body, shivering with tension. 'James and I have never had an affair. You'll have to take my word for it. A close relationship, but not an affair.'

'Describe it. This close relationship.' He had imposed complete control on his features now. His eyes told her nothing, his face was the face of a stranger. He met her anxious eyes coolly. 'Well?'

Olivia sank onto the chair he'd vacated. Her fingers twisted together in her lap, her knuckles showing white. To talk about her relationship with James would inevitably disturb memories that were raw and still painful—stark things floating back up to the surface of her mind, the guilt she'd been struggling to bury for three long years showing its ugly, unacceptable face again.

He was waiting, every silent second stamping suspicion more deeply on his mind, eroding what they were to each other. She couldn't let that happen. The price was high, but she would have to pay it.

'My job always meant everything to me,' she told him, searching for words, not knowing how or where to begin. 'I worked hard to get where I am. I had to, gaining extra skills through night school, pushing, pushing, always pushing. Eventually, I got promoted as high as I could get within the company—personal assistant to James. More money, more security. We needed it, Max and I. He had difficulty holding down a job.'

He'd never had a job, not what she'd call a proper one. Just endless, mindless enthusiasm for endless, ill-thought-out projects, all of which had predictably come to nothing.

She'd grown tired of hearing about them in the end, not even listening to his crazy ideas, certainly not after the real disillusionment had set in—when he'd run through a succession of handouts from his moderately wealthy, over-indulgent parents, plus the small legacy from her mother who'd died a year after she'd married Max.

He'd been so plausible when they'd first met, so full of life and energy, so easy to like. When he'd asked her to marry him she'd accepted, partly, she knew in retrospect, because he dazzled her and partly because she'd had a loveless kind of life and needed to come first with someone. And she'd been lonely.

But less than a year after their marriage she'd seen him for what he was. Feckless. Full of immature dreams and schemes. She'd accepted, then, that if they were to remain solvent she would have to work hard, study, gain new skills, carve out a steady career for herself.

When she'd discovered that he'd mortgaged the modest semi in Islington which his parents had gifted to them on their wedding she'd simply blanked off, not saying a word when he'd explained he needed the money to finance a small publishing company, putting out self-help books written by some woman who seemed to be more in their home than out of it.

She had known the enterprise would fail and had suspected that Max and the woman were far more than business partners. By that time she simply hadn't cared. Just worked harder.

'My job became my lifeline,' she explained truthfully, pushing her silent, secret thoughts away. 'An escape from the reality of what was happening in the rest of my life. And James was—' she sought for the word that would cause the least offence '—understanding. And it's fair to say that I don't know how I'd have got through the period after Max's death without him.'

The truth could hurt. She saw the flicker of pain in Nathan's eyes and blamed herself for the mess her life had been before, a mess which was spilling over and staining her relationship with the only person who had ever truly loved her.

'You must have loved Max very much.'

She looked at him with puzzled eyes. He sounded so bleak. He didn't understand. But then she hadn't told him everything, had she?

'I must have thought I did, once,' she admitted, twisting her fingers into knots. 'He had so much life, so much enthusiasm. But he couldn't channel it in the right direction. At least, that's the way I saw it. Towards the end, we thoroughly disliked each other.'

'You never gave a hint, never told me.' His voice was softer now, drifting over her. Comforting. He stood before her, taking her hands, untwisting her fingers, pulling her to her feet, simply holding her.

The temptation to burst into tears, sob her heart out, was strong. She lay against him, clinging to his strength. He didn't know the worst of it. The worst of her. She hoped he never would...

'I can understand your not wanting to talk publicly about a bad marriage, hon, but this is me, remember? Don't ever close up on me again, promise? Good or bad, I want to know all there is to know about you— I value anything that brings us closer.'

He sat down, pulling her onto his lap, his hold on her gentle but firm, his shockingly sensual mouth wry as he said to her, 'I guess I overreacted to the whole situation, behaved like a fool. For the first time in my life I found I couldn't control my emotions—that's what you do to me! Even hearing your name coupled that way with another man's made me want to punch holes in brick walls. And your reluctance to chuck the job only made matters worse—can't you see that? And that's not an excuse for my bull-headed behaviour,' he told her seriously. 'Simply an explanation. Forgive me?'

Olivia nodded, too choked to speak. He was opening his heart, was strong enough to look his own, very human weakness squarely in the face and admit it. He had probably never been jealous of anyone before and was having trouble handling the painful emotion.

She wound her loving arms around his neck, but he unclasped her hands and held them against his chest, creating a tiny distance between them, watching her closely, ready to analyse every flicker of expression.

'I can understand,' he explained gently, 'why you looked on your job as a lifeline—valued it beyond anything else at that time. You needed a steady income, right? I can see why that happened. But you don't need it now. Not the job, not the income.' His voice was calm, his eyes watching for her reaction.

'You are my wife, your commitment is to me. Always. And I want you with me. Always,' he stressed softly. 'You understand? When we have our first child—and the timing of that is up for discussion— then we'll stay put, grow roots. But until then I intend to conduct my business life exactly as before, and I want you with me—I need you with me. That is not up for discussion.'

An un-negotiable statement, if ever she'd heard one. Olivia held his silvery eyes for long seconds before she lowered her own and mentally capitulated. She loved him far too much to continue this hateful fight over her right to have as much control over her working life as he did over his.

'I want to be with you, too, wherever,' she said with retrospective honesty, wondering now what all the fuss had been about, why her hackles had risen to the ceiling every time she'd faced the fact that he expected her to be the one to adapt. It was arrogance of a kind. 'I hate it when we're apart,' she confessed.

Last week, her first back at work after their honeymoon, had only been tolerable because she'd known he'd be meeting her for lunch every day, and waiting outside the building at five-thirty to whisk her home.

He wouldn't be waiting if she dug in her heels and refused to stop working for James. He would be on the other side of the world and she wouldn't be able to bear it.

His cool drive, his ambition, the way he knew exactly what he wanted and made sure he got it were all things she loved and admired about him, so different from Max's vacillating, light-minded attitude to his life and responsibilities.

And he was right—she didn't need her job, not any more. Nathan wasn't Max; she didn't have to make security for herself. He was her security, her love, her whole world. She could trust him implicitly.

'First thing tomorrow, I'll tell James I'm leaving,' she promised, her breath snagging as she caught the melting, adoring relief in his eyes. He pulled her to him, but she warned, 'There are conditions. Two of them.'

'Whatever.' He was grinning. He looked impossibly gorgeous. She tipped her head back, trying to look businesslike, knowing she failed quite miserably, not caring. She ached to kiss him, her breath coming shallowly, her cheeks flushed. And he knew exactly what she was feeling.

'As you suggested before, I work for you, with you—I've got skills and I want to use them.' She just knew her eyes had gone all misty, and his had dropped languorously, caressingly, to her peaking, tingling breasts, making her go hot all over. She cleared her throat huskily. 'I don't want to be just a pampered doll, to be taken out of its box and played with out of working hours. OK?'

'Done.' His eyes glittered at her, and the corners of his lust-inspiring mouth twitched. 'I'll play with you in working hours as well as out. It won't be any hardship. You know I can't resist. Your secretarial hat won't be any defence at all. Come to think of it—' his fingers found the buttons of her shirt, slipping them smoothly from their moorings '—I think it's playtime now, don't you?'

She gasped, her body trembling with the sheer exhilaration of sexual tension as he brushed the soft green fabric aside, exposing the twin, rosy-tipped globes to his hungry eyes. 'Two—two conditions, I said...'

'Mmm?'

'I work out— Oh!' She tried to ignore the almost reverent way his long fingers were shaping her breasts. It was well-nigh impossible. What he did to her, the way he made her feel, was astonishing, unbelievable. 'Work out my notice. I need to...oh, Nat!...give a month. Um, it's only...only fair.'

'Done.' Slowly, he bent his dark head...

The company head offices of Caldwell Engineering occupied the whole of the top floor of a glass and steel tower on the north bank of the Thames.

Olivia walked through the revolving doors, missing Nathan already.

'I'll meet you at one,' he'd promised as he'd dropped her off. 'The usual little Italian place,' he'd confirmed. Then he'd kissed her lingeringly, and she would have still been in his arms, relishing every blissful second, if she hadn't managed to gather the fraying tatters of her mind together and given him a tiny shove, as reluctant as he to break the loving contact.

'Get moving before you're clamped!' And, anguished from parting, she'd watched him swing away, his movement fluid, graceful as he'd entered the car and pulled out into the morning rush-hour traffic.

She wasn't looking forward to telling James she was leaving and she would miss her work, miss him, miss all the friends she'd made here over the years.

But she would miss Nathan more, far more, if he trotted the globe without her. It was really no contest.

As the lift swept her upwards she renewed the lipstick Nathan had kissed off and exited into the hush of the thickly carpeted reception area. She walked into her secretary's office. Molly was looking frazzled.

'Something heavy's going on.' She opened her big blue eyes very wide and pursed her scarlet lips. 'I've only just got in, early for once, so I haven't been able to pick up much. Just bad vibes.' She glanced over her shoulder as if expecting to see an ogre creeping up on her. 'It's something to do with Mr Hugh. I'm sure of it. He came out of Mr James's office looking like he'd kill the first person to cross his path.'

So surprise me, Olivia thought, but said, 'No doubt all will be made clear in the fullness of time. Just open the post, sweetie, and I'll see what I can find out.'

Please don't let it be a drama, she prayed as she removed her sage-green suit jacket and hung it in the cubby-hole she shared with Molly. Not when I'm only a month away from walking out.

But a lot could be sorted in a month, she told herself as she smoothed the sleek fabric of her skirt over her hips. And if James had finally decided enough was enough, told Hugh to pull his weight or look for another job, then she would be the first of many within the company to applaud.

In her own office she opened her desk diary and unlocked the confidential filing cabinet, extracting the file on Rossi, the giant Italian car manufacturers. She and James were due to work on it today.

Pausing, she looked around. This room, decorated in soothing shades of soft greys and greens, had been her refuge during the last years of her marriage to Max. A place where she could shut out all that was muddled and disappointing in her life, create order and purpose and security. It was here, in her work, that she had found her own identity, proved her worth.

But Nathan was right, she thought, smiling softly. She no longer needed it. She had him, his love. That was all she needed now.

Nevertheless, telling James wasn't going to be easy. The way things were within the company, and in his private life, he could do without the hassle of having to find another PA.

Taking the file, she walked through the door that connected their offices. She didn't knock; they had never stood on ceremony. He might be her boss and a pretty powerful man in his own right, but, more than that, he was her dear friend.

James was in his black leather swivel-chair, his back to her, staring out at the panoramic view of London from the huge plate-glass window. She said his name and he swivelled round slowly, a smile lighting his tired, grey face.

Austerely handsome, in the universally admired classical sense, he was, at forty, only four years older than Nathan. But this morning, Olivia noted worriedly, he looked as if he could be the younger man's father. No welcoming smile could hide the lines of strain on his face, the anxiety in the deep blue eyes.

'What's wrong?' she asked quickly, her heart pumping with fear, wrung with sympathy. 'Is it Vanessa?'

Only she, within the company, knew that his wife was pregnant again. Vanessa had insisted it stay that way. With three miscarriages and one stillbirth behind her she felt, superstitiously, that the fewer people who knew the better.

'No, thank God. She's still fine. Fine, but bored with all this rest, the almost constant check-ups. And anxious, of course, but trying not to show it, poor love.' He placed his hands flat on the polished surface of his desk and stood up, his shoulders tense. 'It's Hugh.' His firm mouth tightened. 'He's finally blown it.'

For a heart-stopping moment Olivia wondered if he'd heard the vicious rumours his brother had been spreading around. That was the last thing he needed right now. If they got back to Vanessa she would be devastated. She had been living the life of an invalid for months now. In her anxious state she might find the rumours easy to believe. In any case, the emotional upset could be dangerous, in her condition.

But, thankfully, that didn't seem to be the problem. James gestured to her to take her usual seat, then buzzed for Molly to bring coffee through.

'I need the caffeine fix!' His smile was bleak. 'Hugh's never pulled his weight,' he admitted heavily. 'I covered for him—don't ask me why. Blood's thicker than water, I suppose. But—' He broke off as Molly came in with the tray, her eyes bright with curiosity, and only continued when she was safely out of the way.

'We've been losing orders, you know that. The whole company knows that. I had my suspicions, and while you were away I had a few things checked out.' He accepted the coffee she passed him with a nod of thanks. 'He's been taking massive backhanders from our rivals, putting in estimates substantially higher than theirs, to make sure the orders went their way.'

'That's terrible!' Olivia gasped, appalled. She had always known Hugh Caldwell was a worm, pathologically jealous of his older brother's achievements, his looks, his private wealth—but to stoop that low almost beggared belief!

James nodded, his head bent as he cradled his cup in both hands, as if he needed the reassurance of the warmth. 'I only got final, irrefutable confirmation through at six this morning.' He pushed a fax across the surface of the desk with the tip of one finger, as if touching it would soil his hands. 'I phoned him, told him to get his butt out of bed and over here, fast. He tried to bluff his way out of it.' He shrugged wearily. 'But I showed him the proof, and told him that as far as Caldwell Engineering went he was history.'

Privately, Olivia thought it was the best news James could give his board of directors. Hugh Caldwell had been a millstone for years. She couldn't say that—James had obviously been shattered by the proof of the depth of his brother's perfidy—but there was something she did want to know.

'This has been building up for some time, you said. You didn't give a hint that anything was wrong last week. Shouldn't you have told me?'

'And get you as worried as I was?' This time his smile was warm and sparky. 'You were just back from honeymoon, radiant, full of joy. I didn't want to spoil that for you. So I waited until I got proof positive.'

Olivia shivered suddenly. Hugh Caldwell had almost spoiled that radiance, that joy, with his vicious lies. She wondered whether she should warn James of the evil stories that would be going the rounds and quickly decided against it. He had enough on his plate without that.

'Anyway,' James said, putting his empty cup back on the tray. 'We've got a busy morning ahead. We need to work on the Rossi deal—make sure Hugh didn't foul that up for us—and sandwich in a meeting of heads of department. Fix it for ten, would you, Liv? Make sure everyone attends. We're going to have to appoint another sales director—young Foster, or Liam Griffiths? Or someone from outside? It will need some thought; we have to get it right this time. So, until the Rossi deal's in the bag, you and I will take the job on board.'

Olivia went cold. As she stood up, her knees felt distinctly wobbly. She pushed the file across the desk towards him and collected the tray, ready to go to her own office and set up that meeting.

Disloyalty swamped her. 'You're going to have to appoint a new PA, too,' she told him remorsefully. Her first loyalty was to Nathan; of course it was. And she didn't regret that. 'I'm sorry, James. I know it's a bad time but Nathan's work takes him all over the world. He wants me with him and naturally I want that too.' She met his frowning eyes. 'I'll work out my full month's notice, of course, and, hopefully, we'll get everything back on an even keel in that time.'

'Not a chance.' He laid his arms heavily on the desktop, staring at the Rossi file. 'If we don't get the Italian order—and that's only the tip of the iceberg— and rake up new business to take place of the orders my dear brother lost us, we're ruined. It won't be merely a question of laying off factory and office workers—and that would be bad enough—but of selling out, if we could, or calling in the receivers.'

'I had no idea!' Olivia sat down again in a rush. She felt winded. They had been losing orders, she'd been aware of that, but not of the extent of the damage. A lot had happened in the two months she'd been away.

'It boiled to a head while you were on honeymoon,' James admitted. 'And we're going to have to work like stink to get back on track. Look—' his eyes met hers levelly '—I'm relying on you. You're my right hand; you know as much about running this business as I do. I need you, Liv. If we're going to come through this I need you with me. Could you stretch that month to six? By then, with your help, I should have pulled it all together again.'

What could she say? Olivia bit her lower lip and let out a shuddering sigh. They had worked in tandem for so long, and he, and Vanessa, had been there for her after Max had died, holding her together, helping her get her head straight. And before that, long before that, while she'd been a humble secretary in the accounts department, he'd seen her potential and encouraged her, quietly noting her efforts to gain extra skills, moving her up the hierarchy, eventually giving her the coveted position as his PA and involving her closely in the day-to-day running of the company.

How could she let him down now?

She closed her eyes briefly, thinking quickly. She and Nathan had the rest of their lives together. What was a mere six months? Surely Nathan would understand when she explained the situation?

'Six months,' she agreed, hoping she was doing the right thing. 'I owe you.' She saw the relief in his eyes and stood up, collecting the tray again, wondering how she was going to tell Nathan about the change of plan, telling herself over and over that he would understand; of course he would. He wasn't a child to throw a tantrum if he couldn't get his own way.

The two-hour meeting went well, with lengthy discussions on how best to tighten up departments, secure new orders—an unusually subdued Molly taking notes—the managers leaving with sober faces to take the news back to their own departments.

Back from the boardroom, James said, opening the Rossi file, 'Shall we make a start on this? We'll need Foster to go over the costings, find out if Hugh put together an inflated estimate, and put in a revised one, if necessary.'

She dragged her chair to his side of the desk, opened her notebook, and they put their heads down, carefully noting areas that would have to be checked, tossing ideas, queries, suppositions back and forth, forgetting the time until the office door swung open and Nathan said coldly, 'There was no one in either of the outer offices. I hope I'm not disturbing anything?'

Olivia looked up, her heart thumping, unable to do anything about the guilty flush that burned painfully on her face. A quick look at the desk clock told her she should have met him for lunch over half an hour ago. She felt awful.

'Nat—I'm sorry. Something cropped up.' She shot to her feet, unable to help herself, even though she knew the haste must make her seem even more guilty—seeing the scene through his eyes, the two of them sitting so closely together, heads bent over the mass of paperwork, almost touching.

But the rushed apology made no impression. The narrowed grey eyes remained steely, the tough jaw aggressive, and, quickly, her tone appeasing, she made introductions.

'Monroe.' James rose fluidly, extending his hand, his smile easy as he put the cares of the day to one side. 'I'm glad to meet you at last—even if you're trying to take Liv away from me.'

Which wasn't the best thing he could have said, under the circumstances, Olivia thought, her heart dropping through the soles of her elegant shoes. But James wasn't to know that, she excused him sickly, watching as Nathan slowly stepped forward to shake the proffered hand, the contact insultingly brief, his tone hard as he corrected, 'Not trying, Caldwell. I've already succeeded. One short month from today my wife will be a fast fading memory as far as you're concerned.'

James looked bewildered, as well he might, Olivia noted, feeling nauseous as the beginnings of anger showed in his narrowing blue eyes. He had no way of understanding the antagonism and was completely ignorant of the lies Nat had overheard, and that he was fuelling a jealousy Nat was doing his best to conquer, a jealousy that would have been fanned back to ugly life by her stupidity in forgetting the time. She should have told James of Hugh's slanderous lies.

But too late now. Both men were almost visibly bristling and any moment James would remark that Nat was wrong, that he'd already persuaded Liv to stay on for six months, no trouble at all—

'We'll have to hurry.' She grabbed Nathan's arm, not at all reassured by the resistance of hard muscle and bone beneath the sleeve of the lightweight jacket. 'I take it you booked our usual table? They won't keep it indefinitely!'

She knew she was gabbling. Her eyes pleaded with James to stay silent, to say nothing and her small hands tugged again at Nathan's arm, but she didn't feel any real relief when he turned and followed her out of the room. Lunch with her husband would be a far from comfortable affair.

She felt as if she was about to walk into a war zone.

CHAPTER SIX

THE little restaurant was crowded, the level of noise deafening. Olivia pushed her pasta around her plate disconsolately. Everyone else seemed to be having a great time; only she and Nathan were left high and dry on a stony island of unease amid the sea of other people's enjoyment.

Not that he had bawled her out for failing to turn up for their lunch date, making him come to fetch her, finding her in close harmony with the very man her name had been coupled with so intimately. He hadn't so much as mentioned it.

It would have been easier if he had. Then the unfortunate incident could have been given an airing, explained, instead of being left to simmer, building up a nerve-racking head of steam. Waiting for the explosion to happen had robbed her of all appetite.

She laid down her fork and abandoned her meal with a defeated shudder and gulped instead at her iced water.

He was being quite incredibly polite—quellingly, coolly polite—telling her about his morning's work, his voice flat and distant. He'd had his feelers out, he told her, describing several of the oblique phone conversations he'd had, explaining his analysis of financial market trends on the other side of the world.

'The way I see it, a manufacturing group in the

Philippines is about to face a hostile takeover bid from a Japanese company. There's no precise data, just this gut-feeling.' He spared spaghetti and twisted it expertly around his fork. 'A white knight wouldn't come amiss, an injection of capital, securing all those Filipino jobs which would otherwise be lost. It's the type of project that excites me. I'm tempted to delve further.'

But he didn't sound excited. More matter-of-fact, as if he were giving a lecture to a bunch of dull students. Olivia resisted the impulse to clap her hands over her ears to cut out the cool precision of his voice.

She wanted him to involve her in the way he worked, of course she did, only not like this. She hated the distance he seemed to be deliberately putting between them. He was treating her as if she were a stranger—an uninteresting stranger, at that.

And heaven only knew what his reaction would be when she confessed to having promised James she'd stay at her desk for the next six months!

'Not eating?' he queried drily, glancing at the undiminished food on her plate. 'Boring you, am I? Ruined your appetite?'

'Stop it!' she demanded tightly. 'Stop punishing me! I'm sorry I forgot the time. I feel bad about it. But there's a crisis—'

'And that excuses you?' He laid down his fork. His plate was empty, as empty as his voice, his eyes. 'Something crops up at work and you forget everything: your lunch date with me, the fact that I might be kicking my heels wondering what the hell's happened to you, picturing you under the wheels of a bus, the fact that I even exist—because you're too busy holding his hand!'

'You have absolutely no need to be jealous.' Her face was white and pinched with misery. 'And I've said I'm sorry. What more can I say?'

Her head was beginning to ache intolerably, and she knew there was worse to come when he smiled thinly, leaning back in his chair, his fingers drumming lightly on the tablecloth.

'"No need to be jealous"—so you keep telling me.' He beckoned a waiter and ordered coffee, but his cold eyes didn't leave her face for an instant. 'Did you tell him that by now half of London believes the two of you are having an affair? You said you had to discuss it with him before I did anything about it, remember? At the time I couldn't help wondering if your insistence that you needed to talk to him stemmed from the imperative to get your stories straight. An exercise in damage limitation.'

He fell silent as their coffee was brought and Olivia scrambled to her feet, her face flaming. She'd had enough of this! Why did he so easily think the worst of her? Had he, in the past, had so few sexual scruples that he thought it was the norm:

'Sit down.' The pressure of his hand on her wrist forced her back into her seat and she glared at him angrily, tears near the surface.

'Why? What's the point? You can't trust me. What's the point in anything?' She was fighting against making a public scene, hysterical misery scrambling her brain.

'Calm down.' His eyes were hard but his grip had

loosened now, his thumb describing sensitive, soothing circles on the tender white skin of her inner wrist.
'I was about to go on to tell you that I realised I was
being unfair to you in letting myself think that, even
for a moment, to confess that I had a cynical mind.
So, what did he say? Does he agree that we throw the
book at his precious brother?'

Still the gentle, circling stroke of his thumb. Surely
he would feel the rapidly accelerated pulse beat?
Translate that, quite rightly, into guilt!

Taking her courage by the scruff of the neck, she
drew in a raw, shuddery breath, straightened her slim
shoulders and admitted, 'I didn't tell him. Vanessa—
his wife—is ill. Neither of them need that kind of
sleaze to add to everything else.'

Her hand was abruptly abandoned on the table top.
She snatched it away, clasping her fingers together in
her lap, biting her lip.

'How very protective of you, my dear,' he accused
coolly. 'But don't expect me to pretend nothing was
said, and sit on my backside doing damn-all about it.'
He pushed his untouched coffee cup away with the
tip of a finger. 'You did, I take it, remember to mention your resignation? Or did the crisis drive that out
of your head too, along with our lunch date? Or did
you protectively consider that he didn't need to hear
something like that "to add to everything else"?'

'I hate it when you're sarcastic!' The cooler he got,
the more cuttingly sardonic, the more her temper rose.
At the moment she felt it was hitting the roof. 'Of
course I told him!' And, throwing caution out of the
window, she snapped, 'He wasn't pleased. But then I

didn't expect him to be. But he understood. James is an understanding man.'

Unlike you, her eyes, her voice informed him. Belatedly noticing the interested looks coming from the adjacent table, she lowered her voice, controlled the tone, and told him, 'My contract calls for one month's notice. He asked me to give him six.'

'And?' His slaty eyes held hers relentlessly, then narrowed to bitter black ice.

'I agreed,' she answered. 'In view of what had happened, I had no option.'

He beckoned for the bill, removing a gold credit card from his wallet, his long, elegantly made fingers steady. 'You had every option. However, you made your decision. As is your right.'

She stared at him, riveted, her pansy-purple eyes wide. She couldn't believe he was taking this so calmly. She'd expected a volcanic reaction at the very least. Dismayingly, she felt excluded; he was shutting her out. They were so far apart they might have come from different planets.

And he quietly rammed her expulsion down her throat as he re-pocketed his card. 'I'll be leaving for Hong Kong, our operating base in Asia, as soon as I can get a flight. Everything's been put on hold for the last two months, for your sake, and I was willing to tack on another month. But not another six. So both of us have made our decisions and there doesn't seem to be anything to add on the subject.' He stood up, his height, his breadth frighteningly formidable. 'Coming? I'm sure you don't want to waste any more time before getting back to your crisis.'

She shot to her feet, threading her way in front of him between the crowded tables, her mouth tight, her head held high. But as soon as they were on the pavement she turned to him, near to tears.

'You suggested we take two months—it was your honeymoon too, remember!' How dared he suggested that their time in the Bahamas had been solely for her benefit? An expensive sop to keep a new bride sweet, while he'd been secretly counting the days until he could take up his real life again. How dared he?

He simply, smoothly raised one brow. Then hailed a cruising taxi. Unable to believe this was happening, Olivia gasped, 'I didn't want to stay on. I didn't ask to! Don't you even want to know what's been happening—why I felt I had to agree?'

'Not particularly. I'm sure you've convinced yourself that your reasons are good ones.' He handed her into the now stationary taxi, giving the address of her workplace to the driver. And Olivia sat, her back ramrod-straight, her face scarlet with outrage, staring straight ahead for the ridiculously short time the journey took.

How could he be so selfish? Why did he behave as if his needs, his opinions were the only ones that mattered? And how could he shut her out so completely—without a single pang as far as she had been able to see? Pushing her into a taxi because he couldn't be bothered to walk back with her, couldn't wait to get rid of her and start arranging a flight to the other side of the world!

Determinedly pushing her emotional problems to the back of her mind, she worked solidly through the afternoon, taking all James's calls and dealing with them, because he'd shot off up to the Midlands to the larger of the company's three factories.

Whenever Nathan pushed into her mind she pushed him back out again. She wouldn't let her misery, her anxieties over what was happening to them, ruin her concentration. She was being paid to do a job here, and do it she would, to the very best of her ability.

The temptation to stay on at her desk, to phone him and let him know she'd be working late, was strong. She resisted, firmly, and, back in Chelsea, kicking her heels, wished she hadn't.

She hadn't been surprised when he hadn't—as he had all last week—been waiting for her outside the office block, ready to drive her home. She hadn't expected it, not after the disaster lunch had been.

But she had been unbearably hurt when she'd unlocked the door and found the little house empty, not even a note to say where he was, or when he'd be back. Loneliness had settled on her slim shoulders like a cold, wet day, dragging her down.

Catching sight of her miserable face in the bathroom mirror when she went to shower and change, she pulled herself up. This wouldn't do. It simply wouldn't do at all! She would prepare the sort of meal that could wait until he did decide to show up, greet him with a smile, tell him she loved him and make him listen to her reasons for agreeing to what James had asked.

There was a plump free-range chicken in the fridge and she jointed it, added vegetables at random, a few generous slurps of white wine and popped it in the oven to cook itself. She was wondering whether to prepare the salad now, or wait until he came home, when the doorbell rang imperatively.

Her first wild, unreasoning conviction was that Nathan had had an accident. That his cold, unforgiving anger with her had made him lose his usual concentration, his normal expertise when handling that monster of a car of his. Her heart was thumping so wildly it threatened to choke her, and her legs felt too shaky to carry her.

It would be a sick variation on what had happened to Max. And that, too, had been her fault.

She forced her legs to carry her, hanging onto the furniture as she got herself to the door. And almost died of sweet relief when she opened it to Angela and not, as she had been so sickeningly sure, to a sober-faced officer of the law.

'Darling—thank goodness you're in! I said to myself, They'd surely let us know if they were going away! Your line was engaged all morning. And this afternoon—no reply. And I refuse to use that thing you have. I don't talk to machines! So I said to myself that if you were out, or away, I could always book into a hotel. So I took a chance and came anyway!'

Olivia plucked the smart leather overnight case from the doorstep, her relief that her sinister, drop-dead-from-shock imaginings had come to nothing making her smile as if she would never stop.

She hugged her mother-in-law ecstatically then, sobering, asked, 'Don't think I'm not delighted to see you, but is anything wrong?'

Her mind steadied now, not boiling over with hysterical emotions, she took in the unseasonably heavy, ancient tweed suit, strands of rich auburn hair escaping from an inexpert attempt at a chignon, the clump-heeled shoes that looked as if they'd last been used during a heavy gardening stint. Angela had obviously dressed in an almighty hurry.

'Wrong, darling?' The bright eyes were wide, then suddenly crinkled at the corners. 'I haven't left Nathan's father and run away from home, if that's what you're thinking! You won't have a wailing mother-in-law cluttering up your spare room for the foreseeable future! No, I left Edward at home doing all the boring bits and pieces and came up to town to shop till I drop!'

Angela Monroe walked through to the sitting room, Olivia following, still none the wiser. Kicking off her shoes and shedding her jacket to reveal a classic silk shirt, the older woman cried, 'Oh, that's much better! I got so hot on the train! I simply threw on the first things to come to hand when I decided I absolutely had to come up to town. Such a rush. But I don't have a thing to wear, nothing really smart. And that's what I need.' She flopped in an armchair and beamed round contentedly. 'Such a lovely home you have here. Small, but fine for the moment. Where's Nathan?'

'Out on business.' Demanding the earliest possible flight out of the country, Olivia thought bitterly, capable of feeling angry now that her awful fright, her dreadful imaginings were comfortably in the past.

He should have let her know how long he'd be, drat him! But she wasn't going to say any of that to his mother. She poured two glasses of white wine, handing one over and taking her own to one of the other armchairs, curling her legs beneath her and asking, 'So why do you need something really smart?'

'Didn't I tell you? God, you must think I'm a nut case! Truth to tell, it's all been such a rush, I don't know whether I'm coming or going! Lovely wine, darling—a Chardonnay, isn't it? My favourite.'

Then, catching Olivia's expression of humorous exasperation, she explained, 'Edward and I decided we deserved a holiday. We haven't had one for years. We're in danger of becoming stick-in-the-muds, I told him, and we decided to go away at a sensible time, like late September when the garden doesn't need such constant attention. Only, shopping around this morning, we were offered a cancellation. A two-week Greek island cruise—top of the range at a knock-down price. Well, we couldn't turn it down and we leave on Friday. So I had to come to town to shop— I can really push the boat out, buy loads of gorgeous things with the money we'll be saving on the holiday!'

She finished her wine and held her glass out for a refill, her eyes sparkling with excited anticipation. 'I'll only be staying a couple of nights or so, but if it's not convenient just say so. I'm sure I'll be able to find a hotel room somewhere, even if the whole of London is crawling with foreign tourists.'

'We wouldn't hear of it,' Olivia assured the older woman, her heart plunging. She made sure it didn't show, though, topping up the wine glasses, smiling a lot, asking Angela what type of clothes she wanted to buy, where she would start looking, and privately and sinkingly wondering if she and Nathan could present a united front, the picture of an adoring, newly married couple, in front of his far from stupid mother.

And, more importantly, would there be the time, the privacy to put things right between them, the time to explain exactly why she'd agreed to stay on at work for the next six months? To beg him to try to understand, assure him that it hadn't been what she'd wanted, that her conscience hadn't let her refuse? Point out that they had the rest of their lives together…?

'I'll show you up to your room.' Olivia scrambled out of her armchair. The carriage clock showed a few minutes past eight already. Where the hell was Nathan? Why didn't he phone if he was being held up? Or was this part of her punishment?

She covered her anguish by picking up the overnight case, leading the way, saying as lightly as she could, 'We'll eat in half an hour. You must be hungry. Nathan's can keep. It's only a casserole; it won't spoil.' And wondered if she could take the other woman into her confidence, ask her to make herself scarce after they'd eaten, explain that she and Nathan were having difficulties, and knew that she couldn't.

It was their problem; she wouldn't worry poor Angela over something that could be sorted out given time. She would make time, make privacy, even if it meant taking the morning off, make Nathan listen to her point of view while his mother was out buying London!

'Oh, this is nice! I do love your colours—so fresh, yet soothing.'

Pale lemon yellow, soft bluey grey, with touches of sparkly white to lift it. Olivia, hovering just inside the open door, accepted the compliment with a dip of her head. 'I'll leave you to unpack.'

But she couldn't walk out because Angela was still enthusing, 'I can see exactly why you bought this place. It's cute.'

Which was precisely the way her son had described it when he'd taken her to see it for the very first time. Olivia compressed her soft mouth, telling herself ferociously that the sheer bliss of that time would return. It had to. She would make it!

'But I can't see Nathan living in a dolls' house for any length of time.' Angela had plonked her case on the single bed, undoing the leather straps. 'It's a pity about The Grange—I would have loved to have you so close. But no doubt the time wasn't right.'

She extracted a large cotton nightdress, gave it a grimace of distaste and hid it away beneath the pillow. 'I'm going to have to buy far more than I thought. It's amazing how one lets one's entire wardrobe go to pot when one never goes anywhere, isn't it? No, in my opinion, the only way to get Nathan to put down roots is to find him somewhere where he has room to move, room to breathe. A family home in loads of acres.'

Stacking her toiletries on the dressing table, she paused for breath, and Olivia got in, 'I don't really think he's ready—'

'Oh, but you're wrong! Nathan's very possessive, always has been. If they were his acres, he'd stay on them; the roots would come automatically. The thing to do, my dear, is to get pregnant.'

She turned round, facing Olivia, who had her back to the door. 'Oh!' Her face lit up. 'You're back at last, darling! How lovely! Am I a surprise? I'm parking myself on you for a couple of days—mother's privilege. Your father and I are going on a cruise and we both need enormous quantities of lovely new clothes! I'll tell you all about it over supper.'

CHAPTER SEVEN

'SINCE when did you set up as an agony aunt?' Sharp-edged, Nathan's voice sent shivers scurrying up and down Olivia's spine.

She turned slowly, imposing a smile of welcome on features that felt stiff and wooden. 'I didn't hear you come in.'

'Obviously.' So dry the voice, but he was smiling. Just. And only faintly, and almost certainly solely for his mother's benefit, Olivia decided shakily. He gave her a long, smoky, unreadable look then switched his attention back to his parent. 'What brings you here, Ma? Apart from a sudden and might I say reprehensible desire to poke your nose in my affairs?'

'You don't frighten me, Nathan Monroe!' Angela grinned unrepentantly. She looked around for a place to stow her luggage, failed to find one and dropped the case on the floor. She glided forward and wrapped her arms around his shoulders, kissing him enthusiastically on both cheeks, smiling contentedly as he gave her a quick cuddle. 'It was me who changed your nappies, remember? Dried your tears and made sure you ate your greens. And I invited myself because, as I told you, we're going on a cruise. On Friday. And I need to shop.'

'I'll go and check the casserole,' Olivia butted in,

excusing herself, and left them to it; she needed the breathing space.

Both she and Nathan could have done without his mother's ill-timed remark. He would understandably believe they'd been discussing the best way to keep him from treating the world as his workplace, to force him to stay home and make babies for his mother to play with!

Closing the kitchen door behind her, she gave a huge shudder of reaction then gathered herself together. She prepared jacket potatoes for the microwave, tossed a salad, and found another bottle of wine, leaving it on the table for Nathan to open.

Since they'd overheard Hugh Caldwell's malicious gossip everything that could go wrong had gone wrong. They called the phenomenon Murphy's law, didn't they?

She added an extra plate to the warming drawer and decided that luck just had to change some time, so it might as well change this evening, with Angela opting for a very early night, leaving her and Nathan with the time they desperately needed to sort things out.

So she'd drop a few large hints about how tiring shopping in London could be—and keep her fingers crossed!

In the event, supper turned out to be a relaxing affair. No one could remain cross with Angela for long—Nathan certainly couldn't. And no one could stay gloomy in her company, either.

'I'll have to get something suitable for Edward to wear.' She was back on the subject of all the shopping she meant to do, and shook her head when Olivia

offered her cheese and fruit. She smiled, patting her
tummy. 'That was a delicious meal, Livvy, dear, but
I couldn't eat another crumb.' Then she tipped her
head consideringly on one side when Nathan offered
her more wine. 'Do you think I should? I've had two
glasses already.'

'It will put hairs on your chest, Ma.' He grinned,
his eyes meeting Olivia's across the pine table. 'Help
you sleep. You know you can't settle the first night
in a strange bed.'

Olivia's eyes held his, savouring the resurgence of
warmth in the smoky grey depths. She knew what he
wanted. He wanted his mother to yawn her way to
bed and sleep like a log, not out of mischief but from
necessity.

Surely that look meant he was willing now to give
her the opportunity to explain her reasons for agreeing
to stay on, helping James, for the next six months?
He would understand; she knew he would. Then when
he left for Hong Kong, some time within the next few
days, she presumed, she would still miss him like hell
but there wouldn't be the added, dragging pain of suf-
focating half to death under the black cloud that was
threatening their relationship.

'Oh, well—in for a penny, in for a pound!' Angela
held the half-filled glass to the light and sipped ap-
preciatively.

'As I was saying, I have to shop for your father, as
well. Of course, he swears he doesn't need a thing.
He already has holiday clothes, he informed me—he
means those dreadful shorts he used to wear. Do you
remember, darling? He trotted them out every year

when we rented that house for a month in Torquay when you were small. Great wide flapping things, down below his knees, and worn with formal white shirts that had seen better days and were only fit for polishing rags! I told him, I categorically refuse to set one foot on a luxury cruise liner if you have those terrible garments in your luggage. The shorts are probably a thousand years old!'

Her blue eyes twinkled at Olivia. 'He's a terrible hoarder. He refuses to throw anything away in case it might be useful one day.'

'I remember,' Nathan smiled. 'The baggy shorts weren't important. What was important in my young eyes was his ability to conjure a cricket team out of thin air. Kids followed him around like he was the Pied Piper, which meant I made masses of new friends—'

'And I made masses of sandwiches,' Angela giggled. 'And huge slab cakes and gallons of lemonade to feed the brutes—not to mention the mums and dads who tagged along to join in the fun! Oh, we had such lovely holidays!' She tuned her sharing smile on Olivia and Nathan reached out across the table and took her hand.

Olivia felt cocooned in love and security right now. Nathan would make a wonderful father; she just knew he would, she thought wistfully. With parents like his, how could he not?

Everything was going to be all right. Nathan had been understandably annoyed with her, unwilling to put his life on hold for a further six months. She could live with that, could understand it, just as he would understand why she had reached the decision she had.

And very soon now she would be able to explain it all. He hadn't been willing to listen before. But she knew he was now. It was there in his smile, the softness of his eyes, the warm touch of his hand. Her throat clogged up. She cleared it.

'Coffee, Nat, Angela? Or would it keep you awake?' As an excuse to break the party up, to get Nathan to herself, it was seamless.

Angela shook her head. 'I'd better not. But you two go ahead. I'll help clear the dishes then toddle off to bed. A busy day tomorrow.'

Waving aside the offer of help, her blood surging gloriously through her veins because she and Nat were about to sort out their differences, kiss and make up, she said, 'There's no need. All I have to do is stack it in the dishwasher.'

The phone rang. Nathan took it, and Olivia added, 'If there's anything you need, just ask. We'll have breakfast together at eight.'

Nathan said darkly, 'It's for you,' and held out the receiver, his face grim, watching her narrowly as she moved to take it.

It was James.

He said, 'Look, Livvy, I'm sorry to ask this, but could you nip over and stay with Vanessa? Just until I get back. I'm in Birmingham and starting back right now. I've already checked out of the hotel.'

He sounded almost frantic with worry, and before she gently refused, because no way could she defer her talk with Nathan, she had to ask, 'Are you all right?'

Vanessa always got edgy when James was away from home and in the past, in the early days of the pregnancy, before she'd met Nathan, she'd stayed with Vanny overnight when James was away, partly because she liked the other woman, and worried for the safety of this longed-for child of theirs, and partly because she owed her and James a very great deal.

'Me? I'm OK.' He didn't sound too sure about that. 'It's Vanny. When I phoned her from my hotel ten minutes ago she was in tears. There's been some bleeding. Her doctor's on his way and I'm sure he'll insist she goes into hospital. I don't want her to be on her own if things—' there was an audible shake in his voice '—things get worse. I'd have asked her sister but she, Jake and the twins are on a touring holiday in Normandy. And Vanny would prefer you, in any case. Liz tends to flap, which is the last thing she needs.'

Olivia went cold all over. If Vanessa lost this child she would fall apart. Out of the corner of her eye she saw Angela wave her hand and mouth 'Goodnight', leaving the room, felt the bleak severity of Nathan's watching eyes and said thickly—because what else, in all conscience, could she do?— 'I'll be straight over.'

'What was that about? Can't he leave you alone for five minutes?' His eyes had darkened to charcoal, threatening. 'If he thinks my wife's going to run to him whenever he whistles, he can forget it.'

'I'm not running to him,' Olivia said wearily, pushing her fingers through her hair. 'It's Vanessa, James's wife; she's pregnant and—'

'You should make notes, make sure you get your story straight—you told me she was ill, if I remember,' he sliced in coldly, pushing his hands in the pockets of his jeans, rocking back on his heels, his mouth drawn back against his teeth in a sardonic grimace that told her clearly he wasn't going to believe whatever she said. 'Since when has pregnancy been regarded as an illness? And what,' he emphasised icily, 'has it got to do with you, in any case?'

'Why don't you ever listen to me?' she countered, her voice husky, unsteady, her temper beginning to run out of control. 'You jump in with your ill-founded conclusions and flatten me!' She turned back to the phone and punched in the number of a local taxi firm, but his large hand took the receiver and replaced it decisively.

'OK, so I'm listening. But before you trot out a hundred and one reasons why you should spend the rest of the evening with James Caldwell you might like to know that these are the last few hours we'll be spending together for quite some time.'

Through the haze of outrage at his high-handed, arrogant treatment of her she saw a muscle clench at the side of his shadowed jawline, and felt as if she'd just been hit by a steamroller when he added tightly, 'I'm booked on an early flight out in the morning.'

So soon! She'd imagined they'd have longer. She knew he was eager to take up his normal working practices again, and considered six months too long to spend tethered to their home. In a way, she understood that, had come to terms with it, but leaving tomorrow... And Vanessa was in danger of yet another miscarriage, waiting for her, needing her support...

'Well?' Nathan reminded her he was waiting, his voice hard, and she shook her head numbly, trying to breathe. She felt as if all the breath had been squeezed out of her lungs, her bones shaking with the enormity of what seemed to be happening to them.

'I've no intention of spending the rest of the evening with James,' she managed thickly. 'He was phoning from Birmingham and should be on his way back by now. And—' she shrugged helplessly '—to women like Vanessa pregnancy is a type of illness. They both long for children but she's already had three miscarriages and one stillbirth.'

She dragged in a long, sighed breath. 'This time she's been wrapped in cotton wool and everything seemed to be OK—until this evening.' She glanced up at him in mute misery. 'The doctor's on his way. James is sure she'll be hospitalised. There's no one but me who can be with her in time.'

She watched his hard face with anxious eyes. 'If you tell me not to go, tell me that if I do I'll be ruining our marriage, or even tarnishing it, then I'll stay. But if you can't or won't believe that I'm not rushing out for a sordid assignation with James, then there's not much hope for us, is there?'

He stared at her for long, aching seconds, then grunted, 'Just get your things.' He frowned with dark impatience, reaching for his car keys from a hook on the dresser. 'I'll drive you.'

'I could get a cab—you've been drinking,' she reminded him, shivering because they suddenly seemed further apart than ever, and she hated it. Hated the way his steely eyes narrowed.

'One glass of wine with supper hardly counts. Just tell me where we're headed for.'

'Belgravia,' she told him woodenly, her movements stiff as she reached for her soft leather shoulder bag. Was he insisting on driving her out of consideration, because it would save time? Or was he suspicious, checking up on her? Could he, in the dark, unexplored regions of his mind, believe she'd been lying to him, telling any old story to cover a lovers' secret meeting?

She couldn't ask him. It would be safer to keep the lid on that particular can of worms. The journey to the elegant town house in its quiet square was soon over and, parking outside the short and shallow flight of steps, Nathan cut the engine and said, 'I'll come in with you.'

There were glints of light behind the curtains both downstairs and up. Olivia could imagine Vanessa waiting, het up, worried out of her skin. She would hate a stranger seeing her like that.

'Or would you prefer it if I didn't?' he asked drily, sardonic eyes sweeping over her face, noting the nervous way she bit on the corner of her lower lip.

The first of the stars were showing in the dark blue evening sky and Olivia fixed her eyes on the biggest and brightest. If only she could wish away the events of the last few days, each one adding to the pile of suspicion. How soon would it be before the pile was a high wall, impenetrable?

She sighed—she couldn't help it—and said tiredly,

'Come in if you must. If it helps. But I warn you, Vanessa won't be feeling very sociable.' There was no sign of the doctor's car yet and her friend would be straining her ears for his arrival, desperately worried that she might again lose a precious child.

His reply was to start up the engine, telling her over the throaty purr, 'Socialising wasn't what I had in mind. But I bow to your obvious reluctance. Phone when you want me to fetch you home.'

He didn't give an inch! Olivia thought as she watched the car shoot away down the quiet street. It was almost as if he knew their relationship was floundering and wasn't letting himself care!

But she was here now, she reminded herself, and had to give Vanessa what support she could. Blinking back tears, she walked up the steps...

'She'll be fine this time. I'm sure of it,' Olivia asserted, echoing the words Vanessa's consultant had said back at the private clinic. 'She's getting the best possible treatment, and there are only another couple of months to go.' She was so tired she could scarcely keep her eyes open. Dawn was breaking over the city streets.

'I hope to God you're right,' James muttered, his hands tight on the wheel, his face grey with fatigue. 'It breaks me up to see her so afraid, in pain. I can't bear to think what will happen if she loses this child. I feel so damned useless!'

Tears of compassion for his obvious anguish blurred her vision and she said quickly, thickly, 'She's not in pain now. And that's an excellent sign, and you're not useless. Don't think it. You're always there for her; that's what counts.'

'Not last night, I wasn't,' he argued gruffly. 'And thanks for thinking to leave that note for me, telling me she'd been admitted to the nursing home. Thanks for everything. She told me she felt a thousand times better after you arrived. I felt bad, asking you to drop everything. But I couldn't think what else to do.'

'Nonsense,' Olivia said, meaning it. 'When I think what you and Vanny did for me after Max was killed, I know I'll never be able to repay the debt, no matter how many times you call on me in a crisis.'

But James merely shrugged, persisting, 'I hope Nathan didn't mind lending you to us? He seemed—' he paused, searching for words '—a tad aggressive this afternoon.'

The big car purred along the Embankment, dawn light staining the smooth surface of the Thames a rosy pink. For a split second she was tempted to tell him about the vicious gossip Hugh was putting around. That would explain everything. But, as she had done before, she thought better of it. Poor James had even more to worry about now.

'He was just annoyed because I'd forgotten our lunch date,' she excused lightly. 'It had nothing at all to do with you.'

Oh, if only that were true! They were nearly at the turning for the mews cottage now, and for the first time she seriously doubted the wisdom of agreeing to have James drive her home.

They'd both listened to the consultant's reassuring words and while James had gone to spend a few more

minutes with his wife Olivia had snatched a quick
coffee and then gone in search of a pay phone.

But James had found her first, refusing to allow her
to disturb Nathan at this hour.

'I'm going back myself, to pack a few more things
Vanny needs and grab a couple of hours' sleep, so I
might just as well drop you off; it's the least I can
do. And why drag him out of bed when there's no
need?'

But would Nathan, with his Hugh Caldwell-induced
doubts, see it that way? Had he been waiting for her
call asking him to fetch her home? Would the fact
that she hadn't phoned him feed his suspicions, make
him wonder what the two of them had been doing
through the long hours of the night?

Clamping her lips together, she cursed the day
Hugh Caldwell had been born. All this mess was
down to him—the malicious gossip that had made
Nathan doubt her. Even though he was doing his best
to squash them, she knew the poisonous doubts and
suspicions kept creeping through. The greed and spite
that had led Hugh to cheat his brother, lose the company those vital orders, meant she'd had no option
but to stay on at work much longer than Nathan had
wanted her to.

The little house was in darkness but the outside
security light came on as James drew up, leaving the
engine running. He put his hand over hers as her fingers numbly struggled with the seat belt.

'Thanks again, for everything.' His face might be
grey with fatigue but his blue eyes smiled at her.
'Take the morning off; catch up on your sleep. Here,

let me—' He moved her hand gently aside and dealt with the seat-belt fastening and, as she hauled herself tiredly out of the car, she thought she saw a curtain move at an upstairs window but couldn't be sure. Her weary eyes were probably playing tricks on her.

Everything was silent as she entered, so the sensation of being watched had been down to her imagination. She eased her feet out of her shoes and padded quietly upstairs, slipping into the bedroom she shared with Nathan, undressing, her fingers fumbling in the darkness, the utter silence.

She hadn't the energy to bother with a shower. Her slim body quivered with nervous tension as she lifted the light covers and slipped in beside him, praying he wouldn't wake. She felt like a cheating wife, and hated it!

And shock made her gasp as he reached for her, dragging her naked body against his, burying his face in the scented cloud of her hair, nudging her thighs part with his knee, his mouth possessing hers in a kiss that was fraught with some nameless emotion.

She wrapped her arms around his lean body, feeling the tension in him, the need that was driving the breath from his lungs—emotional, rasping sounds that were almost sobs.

'Nat—' When his mouth finally relinquished hers she spoke his name, needing to tell him how much she loved him.

But he said thickly, 'No. Don't talk. Hold me. I need you to hold me.'

She held him, stroking the wide, hard planes of his shoulders, absorbing the tiny tremors that racked his body into her own, her heart contracting, her eyes drifting closed as he smothered her throat with anguished kisses.

He was vulnerable, unsure, the lean, hard arrogance of him brought down by uncertainty. He was fighting to believe in her love, her loyalty, fighting the poison of Hugh's gossip, but she, unwittingly, had added to the armies ranged against him.

She had no right to subject him to this; she hadn't meant to; none of it had been calculated. It had simply happened—the crisis at work, Vanny's problems.

Tears filled her eyes and she said fiercely, 'I love you. I love you!'

He tasted the salt on her skin and the tension flowed out of him, as if washed away by her tears, and he cradled her in his arms gently, his warm lips kissing the tears away, holding her tenderly until she fell into a deep, exhausted sleep.

When she woke she was alone. And she knew he had gone.

CHAPTER EIGHT

'NATHAN said to leave you sleeping because you'd been up all night. Holding a friend's hand, he said. But I was going to bring you a coffee—it didn't seem right for you to wake up and find the place deserted. But we can have breakfast together now you're down. He left for the airport a couple of hours ago.'

I know that, Olivia thought bleakly, watching as her mother-in-law hustled around, making coffee, cutting bread for toast. As soon as she'd woken she'd known he had gone. The little house had had that peculiar emptiness that only occurred when he wasn't in it.

But she tried to look bright and unconcerned for the other woman's sake, telling her, 'He's set up some business meetings in Hong Kong.'

And had left without waking her to say goodbye, without bothering to leave a note to tell her when she could expect to see him again. The hurt of it was like a thousand knife points digging into her heart.

'Yes, he said.' Angie popped bread into the toaster. 'So when's he due back?'

On automatic pilot Olivia moved around the kitchen, setting the table. 'I don't know.' And could have bitten her tongue out as she caught her mother-in-law's quick look of sharp concern, and amended, 'He wasn't sure. It depends on how the meetings go.'

Angela Monroe had been a happy lady at the wed-

ding of her only offspring. Marriage meant settling
down, digging in roots, raising a family. Marriage, in
her mind at least, would make her wandering son stay
put. Olivia didn't want to shatter her rosy, cosy
dreams.

'He needs to get his priorities right,' Angie huffed.
'And I told him so. Dashing off for the airport without
having so much as a cup of coffee, indeed! You won't
be able to drop everything and run when there's seven
pounds or so of cuteness in the nursery, I told him.
You won't want to! You should have seen the look
he gave me—it would have blistered paint!'

She put the toast in the rack and poured the coffee,
and Olivia had to clamp her jaws together to prevent
herself from snapping, telling the older woman to stop
interfering, making everything worse. She was much
too fond of her to start what could escalate into an
argument.

'Perhaps he doesn't like being pushed,' she managed to suggest gently. 'Give him time, why don't
you? He'll settle down and be a model father when
he's ready.'

She didn't care if he never settled; she knew that
now. She'd live out of suitcases for the rest of her
life, if that was what he wanted.

She would have liked to have his babies, to create,
with him, a closely bonded, happy family unit, making up for all she had missed. But she would trade all
that without a moment's regret for the opportunity to
be with him, wherever.

She wanted, quite desperately, to explain all that to
him, but he wasn't here. And maybe the damage was

already done. His doubts and nagging suspicions, the possessive streak that had only surfaced during the last few days, fuelled by her own loyalty to James, all topped off with his mother's continual harping on about settling down and giving her grandchildren, might already have damaged their relationship beyond repair.

'He needs a push!' Angie stated blithely, sitting down at the table and spreading her toast with butter and marmalade. 'Come along—don't tell me you don't eat breakfast either! I must say that rose-pink colour suits you.'

'Does it?' Olivia glanced down at her silk robe, as if she had never seen it before. She really wasn't interested in whether that particular shade suited her or not. Not interested in eating, either, but she did sit down and stir her coffee.

And, oblivious to the undercurrents, Angie went on, 'He's had things his own way for far too long, got a stubborn streak a mile wide. You know what it is, of course. Sheer perversity! He considers that anyone born to the sort of privileges he had—a secure and comfortably wealthy background, a first-class education—should automatically get to the top of his or her chosen profession, no excuses allowed! So he has to prove to himself that he could have got there whatever his circumstances. And to do that he has to show that he's always several jumps ahead of the best. If he isn't careful it will get to be an obsession and he'll never have time for anything else. Ridiculous, I call it!'

Olivia didn't think so. Misguided, perhaps, but not ridiculous. She could understand what drove him.

Hadn't she, in a much smaller fashion, done the same thing? Pushing herself to get all the security she could, and never mind the emotional expense?

Her stomach churned at the sudden, swamping surge of guilt, and she pushed the unwanted memories away, brutal in her determined dismissal of them. She bit on a corner of toast to stop Angie fretting about her lack of appetite and made herself smile.

'Shouldn't you be out shopping?'

Angie glanced at her watch, her face sunny. 'I ordered a cab for ten to take me to Harrods. There's plenty of time for you to tell me whose hand you were holding all last night.'

'A girlfriend—she's my boss's wife. She had to go into hospital and he was away on business,' she said quickly. She had no wish to go into the details. Once Angie got on the subject of babies she never stopped, and she'd said too much already!

Fond as she was of her mother-in-law, she wished she'd get ready to go out. She needed time on her own, before she made tracks for the office, time to get her head straight, to come to terms, if she could, with the way Nathan had been last night, the way he'd walked out this morning without saying goodbye. And that reminded her…

'You'll need a doorkey,' she said, changing the subject, unwilling to discuss Vanny's problems. 'I might still be at the office when you get back. You don't want to stand on the doorstep for hours.'

Fetching her shoulder bag from the other room gave her the perfect excuse to leave the table, abandon her barely touched breakfast. She scrabbled through it, finally up-ending it on one of the armchairs because the key had to be there somewhere under all the clutter she seemed to accumulate without even trying.

And then she felt sick, the room going blurred, waltzing around her, the only thing in focus the slim blue and white box that should have been innocent-looking but which seemed like a time bomb.

Her mind had been so preoccupied with the problems she and Nathan were having she'd totally forgotten to take her pills. For three whole days.

Desperately hoping she was mistaken, that she'd swallowed the contraceptives automatically, without registering she'd done so, she checked the pack, her fingers shaking.

But there was no mistake, or only the three of omission. Involuntarily, she placed the palm of her hand on her flat tummy. Even now, she could be carrying Nathan's child.

And he could accuse her of trying to trap him, tie him down, of following his mother's advice and getting pregnant to make him stay home, forcing him to lead the life he believed she wanted to lead, keeping her job on, hiring a nanny to care for their child because she needed to see James on a regular basis!

She could already hear the accusations in her head!

Hard work, and a growing sense of angry resentment because of the dismissive way Nathan had left her, kept her secret worries at a distance. And when they did surface she told herself that she couldn't possibly be pregnant. It couldn't happen so easily, could it? Then pushed the anxiety out of her head.

Angie, who seemed to have bought up most of Harrods, helped, of course. She never stopped talking, displaying her purchases and leaving Olivia little time to brood—to wonder why Nathan hadn't contacted her to tell her he'd arrived safely, how things were going, that he missed her, when he'd be home again.

But when Angie left, the taxi carrying her to the station bulging with the distinctive dark green carrier bags, loneliness crowded in and Olivia pushed it away and substituted anger.

How dared he treat her as if she didn't exist? Three days and not a word. He was punishing her for spending their last evening away from him, giving Vanny what comfort and support she could.

She hadn't known he'd be leaving quite that early the following morning, had she? So what right had he to treat her as if she were a thoughtless, naughty child due to be taught a salutary lesson?

So when James called her into his office seven days after Nathan had left England, with still no word, she was only too willing to agree when he asked, 'Will you come to Tuscany with me, Livvy? I need to re-negotiate the Italian deal, and fast. It's vitally important we don't lose that order too.'

'Sure. When?' She smiled at him, hiding her worry over the way he was looking, lines of strain on his face that hadn't been there before, a gauntness of feature that told of the pressure he was under. 'Nathan's in Hong Kong, so it doesn't matter if I'm away for a spell.' If he could disappear into thin air, then so could she, she decided bitterly. 'When do we leave?' She couldn't wait. The weight of her resentment over

Nathan's silence was making the Chelsea mews house oppressive.

'Tomorrow evening. The factory's on the outskirts of Lucca but we'll be staying in the old town. The accommodation arrangements have been made that end, meetings set up for three consecutive days. Dig out the files, would you?'

She nodded, standing up and smoothing her skirt over her hips.

'Vanny still OK?' She asked the same question each day, hardly daring to in case there was bad news.

He stood up too, walking to the window, looking out, his voice strained as he told her, 'We've been warned to expect a premature birth. They'll do what they can to prevent it, but it's on the cards.' He turned to look at her, his face resigned. 'That's why I want you with me. If I get called back in an emergency situation, you're more than capable of finalising the details on your own.'

'Thanks.' Gratitude for the vote of confidence swelled up inside her, filling the emptiness created by Nathan's uncaring silence. At least she was important to someone, she thought, her lovely features going pink with pride. 'And try not to worry,' she advised softly. 'As long as the baby's fine—which according to the scans it is—being premature is no big deal these days.'

She sounded and looked more confident than she really felt. Vanny didn't have a good medical track record, but the softening light of relief in the anxious blue eyes, the ghost of a smile, the conscious straightening of the broad shoulders were reward enough.

'You're right, of course. There's no earthly reason why anything should go wrong this time.'

Mentally crossing her fingers, Olivia left him, forced herself to stop wondering if there'd be a message from Nathan on the answering machine when she got home, and got stuck into her work, putting Molly in the picture, making sure she had everything she needed to hold the fort in her absence.

She worked late. Very late. James was visiting Vanny and there was plenty to do. Besides, the lonely silence of the little house gave her the shudders. It emphasised the frightening rift that was opening up in her marriage.

She saw the winking red light on the answering machine as soon as she closed the door of the mews cottage behind her, and her heart began beating faster. Nathan?

Cool it, she told herself firmly. It could be anyone. Just anyone. Hateful to get all keyed up, excited, only to be let down.

She walked through the house, switching on lights, hanging her suit in the wardrobe, pulling on an old cotton sweatshirt that just about covered her thighs, and walked barefoot back down the stairs. She told herself she wouldn't burst into tears of disappointment if the message wasn't from Nathan and stamped her hopes right down through the floor because, the way things were going, it looked as though they wouldn't have contact until he walked back through the door.

Her jaw muscles tense, she pressed the 'play' button with an unsteady, nervous finger then released her breath on a shudder of relief as she heard Nathan's sexy, rough-velvet voice.

'It's two in the morning here. I hoped you'd be home by now. Working late? Phone me.'

She reached for a pad, quickly noting down the numbers he reeled off, his hotel and room, searching for warmth in his voice, finding only the rustle of irritation because she hadn't been there when he'd expected her to be.

Had he stayed up deliberately because of the time difference? No, unnecessary when he could have phoned her at work at a time more convenient for him. He was probably working himself, she decided. He could get by on very little sleep.

She wished she'd left the office at the usual time, not stayed on late, burying herself in her work. She couldn't wait to talk to him.

Rapid calculations told her that she had another hour to wait before it would be seven-thirty in the morning with him, and she made herself a pot of coffee, nibbled uninterestedly on a salad sandwich and rehearsed what she would say.

That she loved him, missed him so much it hurt, was counting the days until she could walk away from Caldwell Engineering with a clear conscience and could be with him wherever he went. Always. She would tell him about the upcoming business trip to Italy and promise to phone him as soon as she was back in England.

And, suddenly, she knew exactly what else she was going to do. She would tell James she couldn't continue at work for another six months. She knew how much she owed him, was fully aware of how deep their relationship went, both in the office and out of it. He would see the reversal of her decision as a betrayal but her marriage was the most important thing. She would find time, when they were in Italy together, to break the news gently.

It had happened before. She had put her needs before Max's, and she'd been left with a legacy of guilt she couldn't shake off.

She wouldn't let it happen again.

Her stomach was roiling around in half-excited, half-nervous anticipation as she punched in the numbers Nathan had given her, asking for his room when she got through to Reception. She couldn't wait to hear his voice again, tell him how much she missed him, tell him that she would be quitting work as soon as the month was up.

She wouldn't nag him for not contacting her earlier, much earlier, or for leaving without saying goodbye, she promised herself. She wouldn't even mention it! She needed to reach out to him, to recapture what they had had before—a perfect, exciting, trusting, loving relationship—and she wouldn't have a chance in hell if she launched into recriminations.

When a woman's voice eventually answered, Olivia blinked with frustrated disappointment. The voice sounded sultry, very sexy, as if the owner of it had just crawled out of bed, and hadn't been alone in it, either!

'I'm sorry to have disturbed you,' Olivia apologised. 'I asked to be put through to room five-three-four.'

'You got it.' There was a faint accent there—Australian?—and a definite query in the ensuing pause. Frowning slightly, Olivia glanced down at the scrap of paper in her hand, annoyed with herself for asking for the wrong room number.

But she hadn't, not if she'd jotted it down correctly. Maybe, in her haste, she hadn't?

Swallowing a sigh, she said lightly, 'I guess I got it written down wrongly! I am sorry to have troubled you. Perhaps you could put me back through to Reception? I'm trying to contact a Nathan Monroe who's staying here.'

'You have the correct room.' The woman's voice was now clipped and businesslike, as if she had finally come fully awake, and Olivia couldn't believe she was hearing this, but had to when the voice continued, 'Who shall I say is calling?'

'His wife!' Olivia snapped, then clattered the receiver back on its rest, her brain numb with shock as she stared unseeingly at the instrument. And then she began to shake all over, grabbed the receiver and deliberately left it dangling. She didn't want him ringing back, offering paper-thin explanations. She couldn't handle it right now. Then she fled up to the bathroom and parted with her supper.

She spent the rest of the night staring at a bleak future, not knowing what she was going to do, how she would cope without the magic of being loved, of loving in return, of feeling secure and ecstatically happy.

It had all been a cruel illusion. All of it. They knew so little about each other's past. He had his suspicions about hers and nothing she had done or said had made them go away.

Had his past included a woman to warm his bed in whatever city he found himself in? Did old habits die hard? That hard? Nothing could convince her that the woman had been in his room at seven-thirty in the morning for any innocent or acceptable reason. Not at that early hour, not sounding as she had done initially—sultry, half drugged with sleep, or something even more intimate.

The knowledge was too painful to live with.

'Thank God that's sorted!' James muttered with relief as their early afternoon flight took off from Pisa airport. 'We needed that order. I was afraid, in the beginning, that they'd view the estimate my cheating bastard of a brother put in as a try-on on the firm's behalf. Sacchetti, in particular, took some convincing we hadn't been trying to take them for suckers, losing our bottle at the last minute when we thought they would suss it out and look elsewhere, as too many others have done.'

'But the excuse of a computer error back in the costing department smoothed his feathers.'

Olivia hoped her act of cheerful, smooth efficiency wasn't about to fail her. She'd kept it up ever since they'd left for Italy three days ago, not even allowing herself the luxury of tears or anger alone in her room at night. She hadn't been able to risk anyone seeing the residual pain in her eyes the next morning.

But now a tension headache was building up behind her eyes and pain expanded in the confines of her chest, waiting to explode. To hide it, she chirped on, 'And no urgent need for you to fly home, either!'

James had phoned Vanny twice a day, morning and evening, and reported no problems. Olivia was glad things were working out for the couple. They'd been through some bad times. They needed a break.

There had been a period, a couple of years back, when their marriage had seemed shaky. To James, Vanny had begun to appear as ailing, or miserable, or both. And James had been restless...

She envied them their newly discovered closeness and deeply mourned the state of her own marriage—but she wouldn't let herself think about that now. She didn't dare. She couldn't afford to go to pieces in front of James a second time.

And the act was still in place, though getting desperately thin round the edges, when he parked his car outside her home some time later.

'Shall I come in with you? Check everything's OK?' he offered, and Olivia shook her head speechlessly. It was getting increasingly difficult to hold herself together. While she'd been working with James and the Italians she'd had something to concentrate on. Now there was nothing but Nathan's betrayal.

'You've been very quiet since we landed,' James commented, concern in his voice. 'Feeling all right?'

'Fine.' She made a stab at a reassuring smile. 'Just weary.'

He smiled back at her, the early evening sunlight making his eyes look bluer than ever. 'I wish I could tell you to take tomorrow off as a reward for your invaluable input. But we need to make a decision about a replacement for Hugh. I'll want you to set up interviews, make the arrangements first thing. So, unfortunately, the best I can do is tell you to go early to bed with a good book!'

He hugged her slim shoulders and leant over to plant an affectionate kiss on the side of her face, breaking off, his eyes fixed on a point beyond her head, and sounding acutely uncomfortable, as he muttered, 'You didn't tell me Nathan was back in the UK. He's waiting for you on the doorstep. I guess you won't have any need of a book to take to bed!' His face had gone a dull red. 'Maybe I should come in with you, after all? He—well, he looks a bit miffed,' he understated thinly.

'No.' She unclipped her seat belt, reaching for her handbag from the well of the car. 'Thanks all the same,' she tacked on belatedly, fumbling with the door release.

She could understand what he meant and why he had sounded so uncomfortable with the situation. Nathan was standing in front of the open doorway, his face like stone. He looked like a man who was out for trouble.

She was past pretending in any case, making small talk, making excuses when she had nothing at all to make excuses about.

So he hadn't liked the way James had given her a friendly hug, planted an affectionate, grateful kiss on her cheek. Tough! She didn't like phoning his hotel room early in the morning to have her call answered by one of his floosies!

She had things to say to that husband of hers that

wouldn't stand an audience. She stood on the pavement, willing her legs to hold her upright, while James—understandably looking as if he wished he were anywhere else but here—took her suitcase from the boot. She held Nathan's cold eyes with her own, not even turning as James made some innocuous remark to them both, neither of them responding.

And only when the sound of the engine died away, leaving the street silent, did Nathan address her, his voice lethal.

'Had a lovely business trip, darling?'

CHAPTER NINE

'YES,' Olivia said tersely. 'Though perhaps not quite as lovely as yours!' And she grabbed her case and swept past him, into the house.

He was doing his best to wrong-foot her again, she seethed, dumping her case in the hall and turning to face him, her chin up, heart racing, amethyst eyes sparking. He'd decided to come home just when she'd been away with James, unfortunately, and was making all the capital he could out of the situation, blithely disregarding his own gross misdemeanours!

Well, it simply wasn't on!

Nathan had followed her in, leaning back against the closed door, his arms folded over his impressive chest. Dressed all in black, he looked dangerous. 'Exciting' she refused to admit to!

His grey eyes glittered. 'You refused to talk to me on the phone. What happened? Lost your bottle at the last second, did you? Couldn't actually bring yourself to tell me you were planning a few days away with Caldwell?'

His effrontery took her breath away, made her speechless. He was turning everything round to his own advantage, ignoring the fact that she'd spoken to his bed-mate!

Her mouth tightened as she breathed hard through her nose, struggling to pick coherent sentences out of the whirling emotional mess that was passing for her brain right now.

She wanted to hit him—oh, how she did!

'I arrive home this morning, phone you at the office to give you the good news—' his mouth twisted cynically '—only to have your secretary tell me you've been in Italy the past three days with your boss.' His voice was bitter. 'A case of grabbing your chance while you could? His wife tucked away in her hospital bed, your husband safely on the other side of the world. Why did you bother to phone if you had no intention of speaking to me? Checking I was still there, and not on my way home?'

His face was grim, unforgiving. 'No wonder you're so reluctant to give up your precious job. A wealthy husband to keep you nice and secure, with work that takes him away for great stretches of time, giving you the opportunity to spend quality time with your lover.'

'You have a foul mind!' she said savagely, her heart pumping so fast she felt faint. 'It was a business trip, that was all.'

She made herself walk into the kitchen, her legs wobbly. She put her hands down flat on the table, leaning her weight on her arms.

Her marriage was breaking up around her head and she couldn't believe it. She wanted to curl up in a ball and close her eyes and not have to think about it, any of it, but knew she had to get to grips with what was happening, deal with it somehow.

The relief that she had not—as she'd decided to before that woman had answered his phone—told James she would be leaving at the end of the month was comfort of a sort, albeit of the cold variety. She would need the security of her work now, probably even more than she had done when Max had been alive.

Again, he had followed her, too coldly angry to let go. She wanted to be alone, but he wouldn't let her. Everything inside her went weak, the life force seeming to drain away, and shakily, she reached for a chair, sank onto it, her hand going to her throat.

Instinctively, it seemed, he stepped towards her, a flash of concern in the steely eyes.

'Are you ill?'

She ignored that, asking instead, her voice thick and slurry, 'Who was the woman?'

'What woman?' he countered with terse impatience, and Olivia narrowed her eyes at him. He was pretending he didn't understand what she was talking about! A hot surge of adrenalin pumped through her veins, flooding the weakness out of her system, giving her the strength to be angry.

'The woman who was in your hotel room at seven-thirty the other morning, that's who! The woman who sounded as if she'd just crawled out of your bed!'

'Ah. I see now.' He went very still then slowly rocked back on his heels, pushing his hands into the pockets of his narrow-fitting black jeans. 'My secretary.' He almost smiled. 'Who else would she be?'

'You tell me!' she flung back at him. He looked almost smug and she hated him for that.

'You're jealous.' He hunkered down in front of her, his clever eyes focusing intently on hers. She looked away. He was reading her soul, discovering her secrets, finding her pain. 'She is not important, nothing for you to worry about.' He touched her jawline with long fingers, forcing her to look at him. 'I hired her from the agency I always use out there. she's a first-class secretary. You could have been there in her place, if you weren't so all-fired determined to stay with Caldwell.'

He was swinging everything around again, putting the blame on her. She gritted her teeth.

'Secretary? You're asking me to believe she was working for you at seven-thirty in the morning? Does she always sound as if she's just got out of her employer's bed? You're expecting me to believe there was a purely business reason for her being in your room at a time when any working woman I've ever heard of is still snugly at home?'

She snatched up her hands and brushed his fingers away, her voice rising, shaky, nearly hysterical. But he caught her hands in his, held them.

'You're cold. Such a warm evening, and you're cold. You must be in shock.'

His voice was soft, caring. It made her feel so inept, suddenly, so ridiculously weak with a longing to forget all this, bury it where it would never surface again, lean into the comfort of his arms.

The quick build-up of a sob in her throat was choking her and she couldn't have answered, even if she'd found an answer to give, when he reasoned, 'Yes, I expect you to believe me. Just as you expect me to believe your interlude in Italy with Caldwell was business, pure and simple.'

She gazed at him, her eyes anguished. Could she

believe him? Could he believe her? It was a question of trust, for both of them.

A question she would have to answer. But not now. She couldn't cope with the enormity of it now. And, even if she could have, he wasn't about to let her.

'You're washed out.' He stood up, bringing her with him, still holding her hands. He looked as though he was about to pull her into his arms, then seemed to think better of it. His mouth was smiling but there was not a trace of a smile in his eyes as he told her, 'Take a shower then get into bed. I'll bring supper up on a tray. We could both use an early night.'

Which was exactly what James had advised, she thought dully as she made her way slowly upstairs. Only he couldn't have imagined the traumatic background, although, she remembered, he had been aware of Nathan's black mood, the watchful, dark presence.

She recalled his discomfiture when he'd realised Nathan had been watching him kiss her. Just a simple, affectionate kiss between old friends. But oh, how she wished he hadn't done it! The simple caress would have added volatile fuel to the hotly smouldering embers of Nathan's darkest suspicions.

Why couldn't life be simple? she mourned as she stripped off for the shower. It had seemed simple once, gloriously, wonderfully so. Just her and Nathan and their love for each other, the magical love that had struck in an instant, rendering them incapable of resisting each other.

Everything had seemed so straightforward in those perfect, heady days. All they had needed was to be together, love each other.

It was all messed up now, untidy strands getting in a tangle, questions that had no answers, suspicions that no amount of assurances could blow away, behaviour for which no reason could be given or accepted...

She sighed, longing for those happier times, her fingers edgy as, her shower over, she searched for a nightdress to replace the towel wrapped round her still damp body.

The trouble was, when she'd accepted Nathan's proposal of marriage she'd thrown away her old cotton nightdresses and pyjamas, happily splurging out on sensual silks and sexy lace, the slithery sleekness of satin, wanting to please and delight him.

She pulled the towel more tightly around her, her body shivering. She knew where the panic was coming from. Her body might crave the wonderful ecstasy of their lovemaking, but her mind knew that it would be damaging.

If they made love she wouldn't be able to stop herself from thinking of that woman, wondering if Nathan had been telling the truth, wondering if he had enjoyed her body as much as he enjoyed her own—which one of them rated higher on a scale of one to ten!

And he could well think the same things about her and James!

Almost whimpering, she thrust the drawer back in place, refusing to wear anything that might make him feel the unstoppable stirrings of desire that were the norm whenever they were around each other.

Nathan never wore anything to bed, but he did own

pyjamas, she remembered. In case, he had once told her, laughing, of emergencies. Like having to go into hospital to have an ingrowing toenail removed—as if!—or going downstairs in the middle of the night to grapple with burglars.

She found them, still neatly folded, unworn, and put them on. They were miles too big and, bunching the bottoms up with one hand, she climbed into bed, and was pulling the covers safely up to her chin when Nathan walked in with a tray.

'Shift your legs.' He sat down on her side of the bed, the tray between them. Fluffy scrambled eggs, crisp slices of toast, two king-sized glasses of red wine.

Suddenly, unaccountably shy, she lowered her eyes, refusing to look at him, her fingers nervously pleating the edge of the sheet. At least he hadn't commented on her strange choice of night attire, and she was grateful for that, although she knew that he would have done if things had been normal between them. He would have told her to remove them—or else!

She felt as if they were strangers, not really knowing each other, skirting around each other, a sensation which increased intolerably as he told her about his successful trip.

'I will have to go back quite soon,' he said. 'I left some loose ends. I came away in a hurry when Sasha told me my wife had phoned and left no message,' he added.

Olivia gulped miserably. So that was her name. It was sexy and sultry; it suited her—or the way she sounded, at least.

'Why did you leave without saying goodbye?' she asked hollowly, wondering why she'd asked. She didn't want to bring it all up again; she needed to sleep, to wake refreshed, with her head straight, so she could think sensibly, work out what was happening to them, where their marriage was going. But that didn't stop her tacking on, 'You didn't contact me for days. I felt as if you'd forgotten me.'

'Now would I do that?' There was a smile in his husky voice and it stayed there as he offered, 'I was pretty uptight because you'd spent not just the evening but the whole night with your—friends.' He shrugged loosely. 'I needed time to get over the mood, that's all. Why aren't you eating?'

The subject dismissed, just like that. Disorientated, Olivia stared at him. He was acting so laid-back it wasn't real.

He'd left without saying goodbye and come home to accuse her of the vilest things. And, somewhere along the line, he'd changed. As if nothing had happened. He was treating her as if she were a kid sister, in need of tender loving care.

An impression which was heightened when he forked up a morsel of scrambled egg, holding it out to her, popping it into her mouth, making her eat at least half of what was on the plate so that she felt like an idiot. Then he watched complacently as she drank some of the wine, before removing the tray and taking himself off to the bathroom.

It was still early, only just after nine o'clock, but Olivia curled herself into a sleepy ball. The fraught emotions of the past few days had exhausted her.

But although her body craved sleep her mind was running round in circles, keeping her awake.

Why had Nathan suddenly lost all that anger? Had he decided he could believe her when she'd told him the visit to Italy had been entirely business? And, if that were the case, why was he acting like a big brother, or kind uncle? He seemed indifferent to her.

Her face went red when she realised that was the part she hated most. Contrarily, she wanted him to make love to her, possess her, assure her that everything was fine. And yet she was afraid of it, would always be afraid until she'd sorted the problem of Sasha out in her mind.

What if he hadn't believed it when she'd denied that she and James were lovers but, on reflection, had magnanimously decided that they could have an open marriage? She could get it together with James when he was out of the country, and he could indulge himself with a Sasha in every city! No questions asked in future, no recriminations.

It didn't bear thinking about!

She scrambled up against the pillows, her heart thumping. That scenario didn't fit in with the way they had been, the joy they had found together. It was unthinkable. Absurd!

Relaxing a little, she closed her eyes. They had to believe each other, they had to if their marriage was to survive.

Hazily at first, and then with brilliant clarity, she pictured Sasha the Dedicated. She had to be dedicated, didn't she, to be willing to turn up for work so early in the morning? So she could have no personal life of her own. A big, plain woman with greasy hair and spots—but a high IQ. Or a middle-aged widow who needed to keep herself occupied.

But the voice didn't fit!

Groaning, she slid down beneath the covers again. She wouldn't think about it, not until her head was clearer, not until she and Nathan could sit down together and discuss everything honestly. And she was on the edge of sleep when Nathan walked out of the bathroom and she was jolted wide awake.

He was naked, his hair damp from the shower, and, as always, the power and strength of that lean, hard body made her flesh quiver with sexual awareness, deep-rooted need.

She closed her eyes again, her long lashes fluttering, holding her breath as she heard the rustle of the covers, felt the mattress dip as he slid in beside her.

She wanted him so much she could hardly breathe, yet she knew there was too much to be resolved between them first.

Desire ached inside her, wantonly insistent, the covers and the soft cotton of the swamping pyjamas an unbearable restriction—she wanted to rip them off, turn to him, hold him. But first she would tell him of that earlier decision to quit her job at the end of the month. That would get one obstacle out of the way.

Her breath fluttered and sighed as she waited for him to cuddle close, as he always did, then formed a solid, aching lump in her chest as he settled himself for sleep, his back firmly turned on her.

'Hugh's been putting it about that he walked out of his own accord,' James told her as they broke for a moment to drink the coffee Molly had carried through. 'He was, according to the gossip that's doing the rounds, "dissatisfied with the slovenly way the company's being run"! It's unbelievable. If I had the time and energy to spare I'd take the bastard to court and make him pay back every penny he's cheated out of us!'

But he wouldn't; Olivia knew that. Blood was thicker than water, after all, and James probably suffered from a weird sense of guilt because he'd always had so much more than his younger brother—looks, charisma, private wealth, control of the company. He probably thought that Hugh's malicious, cheating behaviour was partly his own fault!

And Hugh was also telling all and sundry that she and James were having an ongoing affair. Bleakly, she wondered how long it would be before that, too, came to James Caldwell's ears.

She shuddered, thinking of the damage that had already been done to her own marriage, hating to think what it might do to James's and Vanny's. She stirred her coffee absent-mindedly and asked, 'Do you know if he's found another job?'

She wasn't really interested but she needed to keep her mind occupied when she wasn't actually concentrating on her work. Nathan had been in an odd mood this morning, pleasant enough, but distant.

'I won't be late home,' she'd said, poking her head round the door of his study before setting out. He'd brought her coffee at eight this morning, reminding her equably that if she intended to go in to the office today she'd better make tracks. He'd looked fresh, alert, as if he'd been up for hours. And, although his features had been calm, his eyes had been wicked, as if he had a secret he was trying to hide from her.

She hadn't liked the sensation.

'Fine. See you later, then.' He'd turned back to his desk, unconcerned, his voice easy, and she'd left for work, miserably aware that she'd been almost desperately hoping he'd suggest their usual lunch date.

And perhaps she wouldn't see him later at all. He might already be on a flight back to Hong Kong by the time she got home this evening. She didn't know where she was with him these days...

'Not as far as I know.' James shrugged. Olivia blinked, bringing her mind back on track. 'He's still in the Knightsbridge apartment. He's probably salted enough away from his dubious deals to stay on there for some time. When his money runs out he can go to hell. He dug his own grave, after all.'

Olivia couldn't agree more. She gave him a sympathetic smile and saw his face soften. She put her coffee cup aside. 'Shall we get on?'

She left on the stroke of five-thirty, edgy, the late afternoon seeming unbearably hot, making her face glisten with perspiration. Could she and Nathan discuss everything sensibly this evening? Would he come out of that strange, unfathomable, abstracted mood, back to her?

She was so involved with her own thoughts, she didn't see him until he stepped over the pavement and took her arm.

His car was parked. He had come to meet her. Her heart soared.

'Nathan,' she breathed, her face lighting up. 'How lovely!'

He was wearing a soft silk shirt in the same colour as his charcoal jeans. He looked good enough to eat. Slowly, his hand began to caress her arm, his touch burning through the fine cotton of her blouse, his eyes smouldering beneath the lowered lids as he watched her lush mouth.

She heard the rough rasp of his breath and knew he wanted her, right now, and felt her body flower for him and moved closer.

But his fingers dropped from her arm as he stepped away, his small smile unreadable.

'Get a move on. I'm parked illegally.'

That had never bothered him before. But she tried not to worry about it as he drew unhurriedly out into the rush-hour traffic and she said softly, 'I'll cook for us. How about that pasta sauce you're so fond of with a bottle of good Chianti? We need quality time, alone. We need to talk.'

Her eyes were fixed on the strength of his profile, willing the closeness back into their relationship. He didn't take his eyes off the road but said affably, 'Sounds like a nice idea. Some other time, maybe. I've already made plans for this evening and I can't break them. There's someone I'd like you to meet.'

He did look at her then, briefly, with the impassive smile she was beginning to dread. 'OK?'

It would have to be, wouldn't it? She looked away from him quickly, unwilling to let him see the disappointment in her eyes. He would think she was like a spoiled child, wanting her own way.

'Fine,' she said, willing the shake out of her voice. 'I didn't know you'd made plans for this evening. Who are we meeting?' It could be the archangel Gabriel and she still wouldn't want to go, but maybe, looking on the bright side, they'd be home early enough to have that talk.

'Wait and see.' His hard mouth curved exasperatingly. 'I've booked a table for seven; we'll meet at the restaurant. I thought we'd make a night of it.'

Which doubtlessly meant clubbing. And that blew her hope of having time to explore properly the way their marriage seemed to be going right out of the water, didn't it just!

Man-like, he'd gone ahead and made plans for them both without consulting her. Spending a night on the town was the last thing she wanted. His guest was, most likely, someone from the same rarefied business stratum as himself, and he'd expect her to be gracious and charming and sparkly, and she would do her best because that was what marriage was all about—giving and taking…sharing.

They would have that heart-to-heart some other time. It wasn't the end of the world, although it almost felt like it.

'Go and have a long soak in the tub,' Nathan advised half an hour later as he unlatched the door. 'You look frazzled—it's the heat.' He gave her a little push towards the stairs. 'Don't bother to get all dressed up; we're not dining at the Ritz. I'll be up later; there are a couple of faxes I need to respond to.'

'I'm fixing myself a drink first.' Olivia kicked off her shoes. She was doing her best to be accommodating but she'd be damned if she'd let him get away with treating her like a dull-witted child, telling her what to do and how to do it, as he had been doing since the inexplicable sea-change that had come over him yesterday evening. 'Would you like one?' she offered, practically baring her teeth at him.

'Nope.' His grin was lazy, his eyes crinkling. And it was there again—the feeling that he was pandering to a vaguely amusing child. 'You go ahead, but don't hang around. We're meeting up early, remember.'

Go to hell! she muttered inside her head, stamping into the kitchen and grabbing a carton of juice from the fridge. She held the cold surface of the glass she poured herself against the heat of her forehead, cooling herself down in more ways than one, enabling her to take that bath, although there wasn't really time for a good, long soak.

Taking him at his word, she dressed in loose, silky grey trousers topped by a flowing, matching jacket worn over a cream silk camisole. She twisted her long hair loosely on top of her head, because it was cooler that way, and opted for simple pearl drop-earrings for her ears.

She didn't look spectacular, she decided as Nathan marched into the bedroom, whistling. Just coolly sophisticated, so she'd do.

She looked at him in the mirror but he didn't glance her way, so she didn't know if he approved or what she'd chosen to wear or not. He whistled his way round the room, plucking garments from drawers, from the hanging cupboard, padding on through into the bathroom.

An unprecedented attack of modesty? Nathan? She stared at her reflection, then lifted her shoulders in a tiny shrug. She was getting paranoid where he was concerned, questioning every action, coming up with outlandish answers.

He was simply in a hurry.

And utterly, utterly gorgeous, she thought, her breath catching in her throat as he eventually exited the bathroom in a cloud of steam. Sleek black trousers, black shirt, topped by an immaculately cut white jacket. A sexual fantasy come to life.

'You look fantastic.' She went towards him, wrapping her slim arms around his neck, nudging her body close to his, an invitation, if ever there was one, for him to kiss her senseless.

He put her gently aside, glancing at his watch, telling her, 'I've booked a cab. It will be here in two minutes.' His eyes swept over her indifferently. 'Ready?'

He had lost all interest in her!

Scalding tears stung the back of her eyes but the sound of the taxi horn in the mews below helped her to pull herself together.

Get real, she scolded herself as she settled in the back of the cab while Nathan gave the driver the address. He had known the taxi would be arriving at any moment. So he wouldn't have been about to start something, would he?

She lifted her head and smiled at him as he joined her, refusing to let herself remember the time when he had needed no encouragement to make love to her, the time when he would have dropped everything, cancelled anything to have her to himself.

Unsettled, not looking forward to the evening ahead, she made herself talk of little things, inconsequential things, listening to his monosyllabic answers, feeling the tension mounting in him, an excitement she couldn't put a name to. She didn't trust it. She didn't know why. She just didn't.

As they left the taxi she looked at the name above the restaurant he'd chosen and swallowed hard.

Exclusive, expensive, it had a dazzling reputation. It was where the rich and the famous came to see and be seen.

'You should have told me we were coming here,' she all but wailed at him. She would look like a little grey mouse amongst all the glittering designer-wear! 'I could have dressed up for the occasion.'

He glanced down at her fleetingly. 'You look—' his eyes went blank '—very nice.'

She thought his mouth twitched, unforgivably twitched, but couldn't be sure, and she did her best to look confident in her appearance as they were shown to their table. Almost before they were properly seated she sensed a ripple of interest spreading around the elegant seating arrangements and simply stared in unforced admiration as one of the most stunning blondes she had ever set eyes on entered slowly, gracefully accepting the roomful of interest as her due.

Long golden hair tumbled down to her waist, bewitching tendrils brushing her sultry face, her voluptuous body clothed—just—in a shimmering golden fabric that lovingly cupped flamboyantly glorious breasts and ended inches above her knees, displaying yards of sexy silk-clad leg.

The long, shimmering gold wrap she was carrying trailed carelessly along the floor behind her as she made her stunning way towards their table, her big, long-lashed green eyes sending out signals of the come-to-bed variety as the sultry voice with that unmistakable, slight Australian accent poured out, 'Nathan, darling—what a delicious place! How you do spoil me!'

'Sasha.' Nathan rose to his feet, his powerful body full of grace, his eyes full of something Olivia didn't want to see as he introduced her. 'Olivia, meet Sasha Lee. My permanent secretary—as of now.'

CHAPTER TEN

'THAT'S your secretary!' Olivia spilled the words out even before the taxi had started to pull away from the kerb. They had just dropped the sexy blonde off at the wildly expensive hotel Nathan had been using when they'd first met.

It had held such precious memories for Olivia; her eyes had gone warm and dreamy whenever she'd thought of how he'd taken her back there, out of the rain, on that very first wonderful day. Now those memories would be tarnished and spoiled.

'She's staying there?' she accused. 'You must have booked her in! You brought her all the way back from Hong Kong with you? She must be an unbelievably wonderful secretary to justify that much trouble and expense!' She knew she sounded like a jealous wife, but couldn't help it. She was a jealous wife!

'Oh, believe me, she is.'

She caught the slow smile in his voice, the gleam of his teeth in the darkened vehicle, and almost exploded.

'She was all over you—she said two words to me. I counted! And you didn't say much more. You ignored me all evening—I might just as well have stayed home!' She clenched her hands together in her lap, to stop herself from punching him. 'And the way the two of you were dancing was a public disgrace!'

'We took her to a nightclub,' he drawled. 'I could hardly ignore her, could I?'

'There was no "we" about it!' she reminded him hotly. 'The whole rotten evening was your idea. And if that woman knows a word processor from a toaster I'm our neighbour's cat!'

'Livvy, Livvy...' He unclenched her white-knuckled hands and held them in his own. 'It's two in the morning, too late to argue. We both have to work tomorrow. I'm sorry if Sasha ignored you; it was naughty of her,' he said indulgently. 'I should have remembered she's a man's woman; she doesn't have time for anyone of her own sex under seventy. I should have warned you,' he explained lightly. 'Think nothing of it.'

She dragged her hands away. He made no attempt to recapture them, she noted bitterly. He'd had his hands full of Sasha Lee at the nightclub they'd gone on to, fondling, yes, actually fondling the big blonde trollop on the dance-floor when he'd thought she wasn't watching!

Jealousy was flaying her, sending her crazy. That his so-called secretary had ignored her didn't mean a thing. Just that the other woman had no manners at all. But that he had practically ignored her, too, hurt with a pain that was unendurable.

The taxi had barely come to a halt before she scrambled out, leaving Nathan to pay the driver, fumbling with the doorkey and stumbling over the threshold, tempted to lock him out.

She wished she had when he walked right past her, straight into the kitchen, then called her name. She went reluctantly. She felt so racked she didn't know what to do with herself.

He had his head in the fridge, poking around, and he looked up at her, almost accusingly.

'We don't seem to have much in the way of decent salad stuff.'

'So?' She stared at him, puzzled. Surely he couldn't be hungry? Unlike her, he'd eaten like a horse at the restaurant earlier.

He stood up, closing the door of the fridge, his voice lightly dismissive as he told her, 'Don't worry, you weren't to know. I suppose there's enough, at a pinch. Perhaps you could stock up on your way home from work tomorrow? Sasha only eats fresh salad for lunch.'

'What are you talking about?' she asked, her mouth suddenly dry. She put her fingers to her temples. She felt she was going mad.

'Sasha only eats—'

'I know what you said!' she snapped, the steel band round her head getting tighter by the second. 'But I don't understand it!'

He huffed out his breath, then said patiently, 'Did you, or did you not, at one time suggest that with a permanent assistant I could do most of my work from home? And have I, or have I not, decided to do just that? For you, remember. We won't be apart so often; that was the general idea, wasn't it? Of course—' he shrugged, smiling softly, tilting his dark head on one side '—there will be times when Sasha and I need to travel. Back to Hong Kong, for example. And from there on to Australia. But for the next week or two

I'll be here. Which means that my secretary will be here too.'

That woman in her home! Looking at him with her come-to-bed eyes, touching his hand, stroking it, when she wanted to make a point, calling him 'darling', her voice soft and sultry! Nudging her sexy body close to his at every possible opportunity! And Nathan, if tonight was anything to go by, enjoying every minute—and how much more enjoyment would he expect, and lustfully receive, when they had the house to themselves, the dampening presence of his wife out of the way?

Her face went white, pain splintering inside her, exploding, as she got out thinly, 'I don't want her here, in my home.'

He looked at her silently, a long, probing look. Then he said coldly, 'Jealous, Livvy? Now you know what it feels like, don't you?' He pushed his hands into his trouser pockets, his mouth curling without humour. 'Mind you, nobody's actually going around telling the world I've been sleeping with Sasha for years and fully intend to carry on doing so. No third party put the suspicions inside your head. You put them there yourself. You wanted me to stay around more. I decided to humour you. So, like it or not, Sasha is part of the package.'

He was using the other woman to teach her a lesson. It was painfully clear. And the blonde probably didn't know what a secretary was!

He'd been in a foul mood with her when he'd left, suspicious of her relationship with James. Had he met the Lee woman in his hotel, picked her up? Or had she thrown herself at him?

Probably a bit of both. Sex had simmered between the two of them all evening. Olivia had watched it, cringing, hurting inside. Nathan had lapped it up.

'I hate you!' she whispered, and fled from the room.

Olivia woke feeling sick. It was an effort to crawl out of bed, face a new day. As usual, Nathan was up before her, drinking coffee and reading the *Financial Times*.

'Late nights don't suit you.' He lowered his newspaper and looked at her over the top, his eyes silver with lightly veiled amusement, and she glared at him, feeling the gulf between them widening. It was a sickening, bewildering sensation.

She felt too drained to attempt to reach over it; the distance had become too great. Some time in the near future she was going to have to try. But not now.

'Your secretary will arrive full of bounce. I expect that will be some compensation.' She knew she looked washed out and feeling queasy didn't help one bit. Although she hadn't eaten much last night, something must have disagreed with her.

'Yes, I fully anticipate that.' He twitched his paper up, but too late to hide his grin.

'Then I'll leave you to anticipate her in peace,' she snapped, sent a furious glare at the pink broadsheet, grabbed her bag and walked out.

She came back late, having reached a few clear-cut decisions.

Earlier, she'd found herself unable to concentrate on her work for the very first time and, catching herself plotting to hurry back home in her lunch hour, creep through the door, spy on her husband and that woman, see what they were doing, she'd been appalled.

If she weren't careful she'd find herself behaving like a crazy woman—creeping around, spying on her husband, laying traps. She couldn't allow herself to do anything so undignified!

She had to use her brain, handle the situation properly, not let herself get everything out of proportion and not allow the blistering emotion of jealousy to make her act like a fool.

Nathan seemed to be taunting her with the sexy blonde. He found her jealousy amusing; she was sure of that. So the only way to stop it was to act as if she hadn't a jealous bone in her body. He would tire of the cruel game eventually.

Last night had shown her that her obvious jealousy of Sasha Lee merely encouraged him to turn the screw. She would, in future, give him no encouragement at all in that direction.

But if, as she secretly feared and hardly dared contemplate, he was making love with that dreadful woman while her back was turned, or even thinking about it, wanting to, then their marriage was over.

For the moment she didn't feel strong enough to contemplate the horror of that.

And so she trod very carefully, warily, especially after the evening—some time during the first few days of Sasha's so-called employment—when she returned

home from work at her usual time to find the big
blonde swaying down the stairs, fastening the top button of the sleeveless, low-necked, cut-off thing that
Olivia cattily decided was supposed to pass for a
blouse!

'Just using your bathroom. Don't mind, do you?'
The blonde bared her teeth at Olivia's tight-with-
suspicion face, then curved her luscious lips into a
sultry smile as Nathan appeared at the head of the
stairs. 'I'm off now, darling.' She wiggled her fingers
playfully at him, her heavily mascaraed eyelashes fluttering. 'I'll be here in the morning, raring to go!'

'Been using the bathroom too?' Olivia snorted at
him as soon as the door closed on the awful woman,
hating it when he grinned right back at her, furious
with him.

'No. Looking for a list of scheduled flights for
Hong Kong, actually. Can't think where I put it.' He
walked slowly down the stairs, still smiling that slow,
wickedly satisfied smile. 'Do you have a problem with
Sasha making use of our bathroom?' He ignored her
furious face, casually ruffling her hair in passing. 'I
can hardly put a bucket out for her on the pavement
and tell her to freshen up there, can I? What would
the neighbours think?'

He was turning the screw, making no bones about
enjoying the tactic enormously. She refused to rise to
the torment, to give him the satisfaction of reacting
at all!

So every evening when she arrived home she flung
all the windows open wide to rid the cottage of the

reek of Sasha Lee's distinctive perfume. She simply couldn't live with it.

But that was the only acknowledgment of the other woman's existence she made. She was pointedly polite to him—not asking him about his day, because that would involve bringing Sasha's name into the conversation, but telling him, often minutely, about her own. She'd calmly make a meal for them both, pretend not to mind when, after supper, he'd settle down to listen to music through his headphones, effectively excluding her, displaying no desire for conversation.

Just as he displayed no desire for her in bed, turning his back on her, falling asleep at once, as if exhausted by the day's exertions.

Several times she caught herself on the edge of demanding they discuss their marriage, but stopped herself in time.

She had to be calm and collected, not just pretending to be, before they embarked on a discussion that could change their lives.

But the strain of waiting for the right moment was enormous. She felt exhausted all the time, could hardly drag herself out of bed.

Breakfast was a thing of the past and although she usually remembered to send out for sandwiches to eat at her desk at lunchtime she left half of them, her throat closing up in rejection.

She was losing weight and that didn't surprise her. It was all the emotional trauma she was going through. It would have been easier if he'd been angry with her. His cool politeness, those small, meaningless smiles he sometimes gave her, often for no reason that she could see, were much worse than harsh words.

His indifference made her believe he was marking time, waiting calmly until the time was right to explode some dreadful bombshell. No wonder she was reduced to a physical wreck.

And her missed period had to be down to stress.

It couldn't be anything else.

This would be the worst possible time to be pregnant. Under normal circumstances, she would have been delighted to discover she was carrying Nathan's child. But these weren't normal circumstances and he would think she was trying to trap him in a marriage he had grown bored with.

Arriving home from work one sultry evening, she decided things had to change. She was feeling far from calm and collected, but suddenly that didn't matter. In any case, she doubted if she ever would be, and she couldn't exist like this a moment longer.

For once she didn't rush around opening windows but went straight to Nathan's study. In there the air was thick with the cloying perfume, a hateful reminder of the other woman's earlier presence.

Briefly, she wondered if Nathan had ever made love to Sasha in here, or if he'd been insensitive enough to take her to their bed; she wondered exactly what happened during their long hours of privacy.

Had they just jumped out of bed, in a hurry, knowing she was expected home any time, that evening she'd arrived back to witness them both coming downstairs?

The way that woman had been drooling all over him the night the three of them had met had been invitation enough. She might just as well have worn a placard round her neck. And Nathan, she knew, was very highly sexed. He hadn't touched her for ages. Because he hadn't needed to? Because Sasha had given him all he could possibly want?

Her throat jerked convulsively and she pushed the damaging thought away. They were only dangerous suspicions. They weren't the truth, not until he told her they were. Moving further into the room, she at last gained his abstracted attention.

'Good day?' His eyes were bored. He returned them to the pile of papers on his desk, ticking off names on a list with a pencil.

Usually, she would have told him, 'Yes, fine,' and talked to him about it, making her voice light and casual, knowing he wasn't listening to a word she said but pretending not to notice.

Today she said, 'No. Awful.' And knew her words hadn't really registered.

If she told him the office block had been blown up, or that the Queen had visited and she'd been delegated to make her a cup of tea, and the only cups she could find had been chipped, he wouldn't blink an eyelash.

He didn't listen to what she said. He simply wasn't interested.

She cleared her throat briskly and said firmly, loudly enough to penetrate his mind, 'I'd like to go out tonight.'

'If that's what you want.' The wide shoulders beneath the soft white shirt didn't move; the dark head stayed bent over the papers. 'Don't bother cooking for me. I can fix something for myself. Where are you going? Who are you going with?'

He sounded as if he wasn't remotely interested, but had to make some pretence of wanting to know where she'd be. He was adept at piling hurt on top of hurt until she thought her heart would break beneath the weight of it.

'I would like to eat out, with you,' she stated clearly, snatching at her lost equilibrium. 'It would be nice not to have to cook tonight. It's so hot.'

It would be nice to get away from here, just for an hour or two, just the two of them. Away from the constant reminder of the other woman's presence in his life. And gently, over a relaxing meal, she could introduce the subject of their marriage, and what was going wrong with it. Remind him of how things had been when they'd first met, the immediacy of their falling in love.

He had been in love with her. He hadn't been pretending; the emotion had run too deep. It had taken them both over, shattering them with its strength, leaving them clinging to each other.

He did turn round and look at her then, his face blank. Under his unwavering scrutiny, Olivia felt her face go hot. She pushed the heavy fall of hair away from her damp forehead and tried to smile, her face going stiff when he drawled, 'I've got too much on at the moment. Sasha and I didn't get through as much as I thought we might today.'

He swung back to his paperwork. 'Why don't you

put your feet up? Pour yourself a drink. If you don't feel like cooking I'll make the supper, later.'

Dismissed. Just like that. Dismissed, but unable to move.

Why hadn't he and his so-called secretary worked well enough today? Because they'd been otherwise occupied?

The steel band round her chest snapped. Her voice snapped.

'Are you having an affair with that woman?'

'What makes you ask?'

He didn't turn to face her. Because he couldn't look her in the eye and lie to her? Because he wasn't ready, yet, to admit it?

'I would have thought the answer to that was perfectly obvious!'

She would force him, willing or not, to face her. She marched over to his desk and planted her hands on her slender hips, perspiration making the thin cotton of her blouse stick to her body.

'No, not to me it isn't.' His eyes flicked up to her then straight back to his papers and Olivia stuck her small chin out.

'Then you have told her that her job finishes the moment I quit Caldwell's and take her place? Does she know it's a temporary arrangement?'

His answer would be important.

If he had told that dreadful woman she would only be working with him until his wife could take her place, it would mean that he still regarded their marriage, their partnership, as valid, despite the present difficulties. It would mean that, quite possibly, he had picked the sexiest secretary he could find to torment her, that his relationship with Sasha Lee had nothing to do with adultery.

But if he hadn't?

'You're getting hysterical,' he informed her, his voice dry and cool. 'Why don't you do as I suggested and put your feet up?'

'Have you told her?' Olivia persisted. She wasn't hysterical, nowhere near. Suddenly, she felt icily calm, as if she were in the silent eye of a raging storm.

He sighed and tossed his pencil down on the desk. 'No. I haven't. Why should I? You might change your mind, or Caldwell could change it for you.' He paused, his mouth thinning. 'Again.'

She had her answer.

Her face went ashen. She turned smartly on her heels and walked out of the room, her back ramrod-straight. However he dressed it up, he had no intention of getting rid of Sasha Lee—she was sexy, exciting, fun to be around.

And she knew it wouldn't be long before he told her that his secretary would be accompanying him back to Hong Kong to tie up loose ends on the Filipino deal, and then on to Australia.

He had already warned her that it would happen. How long would it be before he decided she no longer had any place in his life? Even less than she had at the moment. Which was little enough.

Still icily calm, she went to the bathroom. There was just one thing left to do before she could decide what was going to happen about her marriage.

She couldn't hold Nathan if he didn't want to be held. She wouldn't want to try.

If it was over she was going to have to drag herself together, look her lonely future squarely in the eye and get on with it. Learn to live with the indescribable pain of losing him.

But first...

She reached to the back of the medicine cabinet and took the pregnancy testing kit out with stiff, cold fingers. She felt as if all her actions were being performed in slow motion.

Bought days ago, she hadn't had the courage to use it until now. Although courage no longer came into it. She was acting, thinking mechanically, like a robot. Robots didn't have feelings, did they?

Ten minutes later all that had changed, the whole world had changed, and she was a shaking bundle of profound emotion.

She was carrying Nathan's child!

White-faced, she walked unsteadily into the bedroom and sat on the edge of the mattress, trembling all over. Part of her exulted in the beautiful knowledge. Part of her was deeply afraid.

Already she loved the tiny scrap of life inside her, would love his child to the end of her life.

But would Nathan feel the same way? Would he think she was trying to trap him?

As far as Nathan was concerned, children were something to look forward to in the future. He had too much drive, too much ambition to clutter his life with them at the moment. Which was why he'd been so uncharacteristically brutal with Angie when she'd tried to twist his arm over viewing The Grange, pointing out that they'd need a much larger home when her grandchildren began to arrive.

He didn't want to tie himself down to a country estate, a house full of children. Certainly not at this stage of his life—his attitude at the time had told her that much. And that had been before their marriage had started to disintegrate.

She shuddered uncontrollably, tears sliding down her pale cheeks.

There was no option, at this point, but to keep her secret to herself. Her pregnancy wouldn't be noticeable for some months to come. That would give Nathan plenty of time to decide whether he still wanted her or not, whether he was too entranced by the sultry Sasha to want to hold onto what was left of his marriage.

What she would never do was hold this precious, coming child as a bargaining counter. She couldn't bear it if he decided to try to make their marriage work just because he was going to be a father.

She wanted all his love. Or nothing at all. She would hate it if she felt he had decided to take the honourable course, to settle down and grin and bear it.

He had to be free to make his own mind up about their future. If she told him about the baby she would take away that freedom.

She dropped her head in her hands, her hair falling about her in a shimmering black cloud. And heard the door open, Nathan's voice.

'Livvy, hon, this can't go on.' His tone was rough-

edged, urgent. 'I'm afraid I've got one hell of a confession to make.' He sounded suddenly soberly con-
trite, desperately uneasy. She had never heard that
note in his voice before. 'You'll probably hate me for
it, and deservedly so. But promise me you'll listen?
Try, at least, to understand?'

Shocked, she looked up at him swiftly, her head
swimming, the little colour she had draining right out
of her face.

He was going to come straight out with it, tell her
about his affair with Sasha, tell her he didn't want her
in his life, say the dreadful words that would end their
marriage; she just knew it! What else could he possibly have to confess?

She put her hand to her heart, as if trying to hold
it together, stop it beating its way right out of her
chest and splintering into a million pieces.

There was a roaring in her ears and she couldn't
see him properly. Her vision was blurred.

But she did sense him move swiftly towards her,
heard the wrenching concern in his voice as he said
raggedly, 'You're ill! Tell me what's wrong!'

She shook her head, incapable of speech, needing
all her will-power to stop herself from fainting. His
brows drew together in a formidable frown as he
pushed her tumbled hair back off her face then lifted
her back against the heaped pillows.

'I'll fetch you some water. If you don't feel a hundred per cent better inside two minutes I'm calling the
doctor.' He touched her clammy forehead with the
tips of his cool fingers, swearing softly, under his
breath, his words inaudible.

Her head clearing a little, she watched him stride into the bathroom for water. She irritated him. That had been made plain to her, swearing like that, under his breath. He had decided to confess his affair with Sasha and her fainting fit had stopped him.

But it wouldn't stop him for long. Unless she went into a coma for the rest of her life, she was going to have to listen.

Within seconds he was back, his face white with a terrible anger.

'When were you going to tell me the good news?'

'I'm sorry?' She licked her parched lips, her brows drawing together over her troubled amethyst eyes, not knowing what he was talking about, flinching at the fury in his eyes. And then she remembered the testing kit, the evidence she'd left on the counter, and her face went scarlet.

'Penny dropped?' he asked contemptuously. 'Is it my child? Or Caldwell's?'

CHAPTER ELEVEN

OLIVIA looked at Nathan as if she didn't know him. 'How dare you ask that?' she demanded thinly. 'How dare you?'

He gave her a long look. 'How convincing you can be when you try, when your back's against the wall!' He paced the room with long, slow strides. 'We can look at it two ways. You took my mother's advice and got pregnant in an attempt to root me in one spot. Which would mean that the gossip is wrong, that you aren't having an affair with Caldwell. You wouldn't want me permanently around if you wanted to spend time with him.' He stopped in his tracks, his eyes lancing her. 'Or the pregnancy was an accident. Well?'

It was useless to try to reason with him. He was capable of thinking the very worst of her. He would spend the rest of his life doubting the parentage of his child, or believing her selfish enough to deliberately get pregnant to tie him down, get her own way.

She shivered, suddenly cold to her bones. Her warm and loving future had been taken away from her. And yet she had his child to love. She would make that enough.

'It was an accident,' she stated coldly.

Which was the truth. She couldn't lie about a thing like that. And she couldn't save their marriage now, no matter what she said. He had been about to confess his affair with Sasha, ask for his freedom. She wouldn't use their child to hold him.

It was over. She could read it in his face. And the shrill of the telephone at the side of the bed almost came as a reprieve.

If it was Sasha, ringing to find out if he'd told his wife about them, made the confession he'd started out on, she would take great pleasure in telling her to go to hell.

But it wasn't. The pent-up determination washed out of her face as she sighed, 'James. What can I do for you?' and watched Nathan stride out of the room, slamming the door behind him.

'You and I are having an affair! It's been going on for years,' James said hoarsely. 'That's according to the gossip one of Vanny's so-called friends passed on to her.'

'Oh, hell! I was afraid of that!' Olivia gripped the receiver tightly, her voice sharp with anxiety. This was the last thing Vanny needed to hear, especially now, shut away from everyone in her hospital bed, worrying over whether she would carry her baby full-term.

Protectively, she placed a hand on her own flat tummy as James blistered, 'You knew about it! You didn't tell me! You should have done! I could have warned her, discussed it with her and put her mind at rest, found out who started it. As it is, she won't listen to a word I say.'

'I've known about it for a long time,' she sighed

wretchedly. 'Nathan heard it too. It hasn't done our marriage much good either.'

'I can imagine,' James came back drily. 'I can understand now why Nathan looks as if he'd like to punch me whenever we meet. So why didn't you tell me what people were saying? You must have known we'd get to hear it sooner or later.'

She hadn't looked that far ahead and she recognised her mistake now. Hadn't Nathan tried to insist they bring James, at least, into it? Do something about it? And she had refused. Which wouldn't have helped him believe in her innocence. But selfishly, she recognised miserably, she had been anxious that her own dreadful guilt shouldn't be made public knowledge.

'I honestly thought I was doing the right thing at the time,' she explained tiredly. 'Sticking my head in the sand and hoping you wouldn't hear the gossip. I thought you'd got enough to contend with as it was— Hugh, the business, Vanny's condition. I believed I was protecting you both.'

Protecting herself, too, she thought sickly. But that hadn't been her prime concern, surely? She couldn't think that badly of herself.

She had been genuinely trying to protect James, and Vanny especially. She hadn't looked far enough ahead and, worst of all, she hadn't looked at it properly from Nathan's point of view. She had expected him to trust her implicitly.

'OK. I'll buy that.' His tone warmed, then took on an edge of deep anxiety. 'Do something for me? Talk to Vanny, tell her you and I have never had an affair, put her mind at rest. I've just come from the hospital; she's in a terrible state. She refused to see me at first, and when she did agree she wouldn't listen to a thing I said. She began to get labour pains—real or imaginary—and started to panic. Do that for me, Liv, would you? For old times' sake?'

He was calling in the debt. After Max's death she had needed him, and he'd been there for her, holding her together. Vanny, too.

'I'll do my best,' she promised, and replaced the receiver, her brows drawn together. Why should Vanessa listen to her reassurances when she'd dismissed James's out of hand? Vanny would expect her to deny everything, wouldn't she?

There was only one person who had the remotest chance of convincing Vanessa and that was her brother-in-law, the man who had once felt enough for her to take her home to meet his family. The man who had started the malicious gossip.

Hoping that Hugh Caldwell, bitter, ejected from the family business, would do the right thing was a long shot, she thought, slipping back into her shoes and collecting her bag. But she had to try.

James had told her Hugh was still at his Knightsbridge apartment and it was early enough for him to be there and not in one of his usual drinking haunts. She slipped quietly down the stairs, the silence of the little house wrapping her body with ice.

She wouldn't tell Nathan where she was going, or even that she was going anywhere. It would only involve her in lengthy explanations, explanations he probably wouldn't be interested in anyway.

He was probably still furious, brooding about the unwelcome fact of her pregnancy, wondering how it would affect his relationship with Sasha, wishing he'd had the opportunity to get his confession out of the way before he'd discovered the evidence of her bombshell.

She picked up a taxi on the Embankment and sat in the back, turning the problem over in her mind. What would be the best approach to take? Appeal to his better nature, if he had one? Threaten him?

But she had nothing to threaten him with, had she? So it was back to his doubtful better nature. Too late, she wished she'd told James exactly who had started the gossip, told him of her intentions. He might have been able to bring some pressure to bear...

Her decision to appeal to Hugh had been instinctive and, typically, she'd jumped up immediately and acted on it, without taking time to see if there were alternatives. All her life she'd been making her own decisions, getting by as best she could. All her life she'd had to rely on herself, and the habit was hard to shake off.

And at least, she thought with shaky humour as the taxi drew up outside the apartment block, thinking about how best to approach Hugh Caldwell, make him undo the mess of misery he had created, had momentarily taken her mind off the breakdown of her own marriage.

She was going to have to face Nathan, though. As soon as she'd done what she could here she would go back to Chelsea and they would sit down together, calmly, and discuss their future.

If he wanted to be with Sasha, and she was sick-eningly certain of it—what else could he possibly have had to confess?—then she would do nothing to stop him. And she would never, ever prevent him see-ing his child. She would make sure he understood that. He hadn't been overjoyed at the thought of fatherhood, but she knew he would love his child. The news had come at a bad time for him, for them both.

Olivia shook her head, blinking. She was wasting time. Her heart was heavy with misery as her sur-roundings came back into focus, the heat of the day still reflecting back up from the paving-stones, the sound of traffic, the slam of a car door.

She forced herself over to the discreet, elegant door, scanned the panel for the correct bell and pressed it, having little hope of achieving her objec-tive, but knowing she at least had to make the attempt before seeing Vanessa herself, and felt her arm taken roughly, shaken.

'So this is the private love-nest? He only has to call and you go running!'

'Nathan!' she gasped. 'Why are you here?' His face was like granite, menacing; he had never seemed so unapproachable.

He looked at her, narrow-eyed. 'If you want me to make myself scarce, forget it. He calls and you run. I wanted to see where you were going for myself. I followed you.'

A disembodied male voice spoke on the intercom and Olivia, her eyes bruised and hunted, shot a fren-zied glance at Nathan and spoke back shakily. 'It's Olivia. I need to speak to you.'

She pushed on the door and Nathan dropped his hand from her arm, as if he couldn't bear that small physical contact, but he followed her like a dark, unshakeable shadow. Thankfully, Hugh's was a ground-floor apartment. She couldn't have made it up the stairs.

More than anything, she wanted to lean against his firm, lean body, gather some of his strength, but knew he didn't want her to touch him.

Pausing outside the door to the apartment, she turned to him. It seemed airless in here and her heart was leaping around like a landed fish. She could scarcely breathe because her love for him, despite his infatuation with Sasha Lee, was pulling her to shreds.

'This isn't what you think at all.' She put out a hand to touch his sleeve and quickly withdrew it. The harsh lines of his beloved face told her he wanted no closeness, not now, not ever. She swallowed thickly, her eyes bright with tears. 'James phoned to tell me that Vanny had heard the gossip about him and me. She—she took it very badly. He wanted me to reassure her—'

'How thoughtful of him,' he cut in, ice in his eyes. 'She's here, is she? You told me she was languishing in a hospital bed somewhere.'

'No, but Hugh is.' She shook her head, tears falling now, spilling down her cheeks. 'He started the gossip. I thought he'd be the best person to put things right. She wouldn't listen to James. Why should she listen to me?'

He gave her no answer but the look in his eyes was pointed. Why, indeed? he seemed to be thinking and she told him chokily, 'I couldn't bear it if she lost the baby. I couldn't have that on my conscience.'

'There's a danger of that?' His mouth was grim.

Olivia nodded, her soft lips trembling. 'With her past history, the state she's in now—'

'So why doesn't your precious James force his brother to try to put things right?'

'Because he doesn't know, yet, who spread the gossip,' she excused miserably.

'Then we'll have to make the bastard tell her he was lying, whether he was or not.' His words were staccato. 'Why should an innocent woman have to suffer?' Because of her husband's misdemeanours, his tone implied.

His clenched fist thundered against the smooth wood panels of the door and Olivia shuddered. He made her feel as if she was some kind of low-life, she thought bitterly, following unsteadily as he pushed open the door and walked in and Hugh appeared in the vestibule, his thickening body dressed for a night out on the town in dinner jacket and black tie.

'So.' His mouth was a sneer, his little eyes antagonistic. 'Olivia. What an unexpected pleasure. Unfortunately, I can give you five minutes only. A social engagement, you understand.'

'You will give us exactly as long as we need,' Nathan said coldly, and Olivia watched the other man shrivel up inside his expensive suit as he took in the dark menace that was Nathan Monroe for the first time.

She would have found it funny if her heart hadn't been breaking and could only stare, marvelling at

Nathan's silent power, as Hugh, his little feet in their highly polished shoes pattering backwards, invited belatedly, 'Perhaps you'd better come in.'

'No need. My wife can say what she needs to here.' His eyes swept dismissively over the white-painted vestibule, the thick blue carpet, gilded chairs flanking a small wall table. 'Olivia?'

He was inviting her to say her piece, his tone sharp, indicating that he wanted it out of the way, wanted to expel contaminated air from his lungs. But her throat felt tight, her tongue thick in her mouth. She dragged her eyes from the overfed, over-indulged face in front of her and looked appealingly into Nathan's harsh eyes.

He frowned impatiently down at her, then took over. 'You've been spreading gossip, Caldwell. And don't try to deny it; I was there. I heard it. I wanted to push your teeth through the back of your head—' his mouth curled thinly '—but for reasons best known to herself my wife dissuaded me. But right now—' he took a step forward '—there is no power on earth that will prevent me from doing just that—' another step took him closer to the now visibly cringing figure '—unless you do exactly as I say.'

Hugh Caldwell shot a frenzied look in Olivia's direction, as if hoping she would somehow save him again, saw the utter contempt in her eyes and muttered, 'What is it you want, then? I don't know what you're talking about.'

'We're talking about your telling anyone who'd listen that I killed Max then jumped into bed with James, and have been there, on and off, ever since!' Olivia snapped, suddenly despising herself for the spineless way she'd behaved ever since Nathan had shown up on the doorstep.

But his unexpected appearance, the way he had followed her, had brought her misery back in waves, swamping her, driving all she had decided to say clean out of her head.

Nathan gave her a long, level, sideways look before saying, grim determination edging his voice, 'Whatever you believe, or think you believe, you will go to your sister-in-law now. You will put her mind at rest. Tell her you started the rumours, tell her you lied. She is expecting a child, as presumably you know. I'm told she may well lose it because of the upset. Even if there's no real danger of that happening, do you think it's acceptable for an entirely innocent woman to be made to suffer?'

'And if I won't?' Hugh's beady eyes were wary, even though he blustered. He was obviously wriggling, trying to escape. He wouldn't want to admit anything.

And Nathan said softly, almost pleasantly, 'Then I will take you apart, piece by piece.'

He meant it; he really meant it.

Olivia shuddered. She hated violence in any form. She had good reason to. Nathan wasn't normally violent. The evil rumours this disgusting, mean-minded man had started had been responsible for the initial breakdown of their marriage. That Sasha Lee had stepped in and taken over, providing him with single-minded adoration, not a divided loyalty in sight, would be neither here nor there in Nathan's opinion.

It was a symptom of the disease Caldwell had infected their marriage with.

Hugh Caldwell had been responsible for the beginning of the rot, ruining something precious that could never be regained, and he would be the recipient of Nathan's blistering rage.

Hugh visibly crumpled, his face going grey. But he wasn't giving up entirely.

'There's no need to get nasty. I'll do what I can, even if it does mean telling lies. I've always been fond of Vanny. A lovely girl, wasted on that—'

A black look from Nathan, a look of unadulterated warning, had him almost tripping over himself in his rush for the door, squeezing himself between the two of them. But he couldn't resist a final gibe, his resentment at the way Olivia had treated his heavy pass with the contempt it deserved all those years ago surfacing, flooding his eyes with spite as they locked with hers.

'We both know the truth, don't we, Olivia? There's one part of what I said that is the undoubted, absolute truth,' he sneered. 'Isn't there? So what do you say? Guilty or innocent?'

Olivia stared at him, hating him. Nathan was very still, as if he was holding his breath, waiting for her to answer, to deny everything.

A dull throbbing started up behind her eyes, tears stinging them. Tears of regret. Tears for the past. Tears for the love she had lost.

There was no point in hiding behind denials. Her marriage was over. Nathan couldn't think more badly of her than he did now. And perhaps admitting her guilt, in front of the man she loved more than her life, would be expiation of a kind.

She had no real idea how Hugh Caldwell had come by his knowledge. Unless he had listened at doors, peeped round corners, heard and seen what had passed between her and James...

She hung her head, her face white, her world spinning toward its end.

'Guilty,' she whispered.

Hugh Caldwell sniggered.

Nathan hit him.

CHAPTER TWELVE

THROUGH the glass doors Olivia saw Hugh Caldwell slinking out, one eye already turning purple in his pale and shaken face. On the other side of the flower-scented waiting room Nathan was standing at one of the long windows, staring out.

She didn't know how to break the silence, tell him that Hugh had gone, that his part in this was over. She shivered, wrapping her arms around her body. The coldness came from inside her. She would never feel properly warm, fully alive again.

Nathan had picked Hugh up off the floor and hustled him out into his car, pushing him into the back, tersely asking Olivia which hospital Vanny was in as he got in beside her, his face white, uncompromisingly grim.

Olivia didn't know how much had been achieved. Hugh had been with Vanny, with James in attendance, for a little over twenty minutes.

James's eyebrows had shot up to his hairline when the three of them had arrived, and Olivia had babbled, 'We thought Hugh was the only person who could put things right. He started the rumours. He's going to do what he can. How is she?'

James had dragged his contemptuous eyes from his brother's sulky face.

'More settled. She's been given a couple of injec-

169

tions.' He'd glanced witheringly at Hugh. 'Why didn't I guess you were behind it all? If you foul up on this—'

'He won't.' Nathan had spoken for the first time, his tone a dark warning, and James had given him a quick, admiring look before pushing his brother in front of him down the silent, carpeted corridor.

Not speaking, she and Nathan had gravitated to the waiting room. As a privately run hospital it offered every comfort. Softly upholstered chairs, up-to-date glossy magazines, hot coffee in a heated glass jug— everything to keep a visitor or a patient waiting for an appointment occupied.

But Nathan had stationed himself in front of one of the windows, his body rigid, his thoughts kept closely to himself, while she had stood in front of the double glass doors. Waiting.

She had seen one of the nursing staff and then Hugh, and she didn't know what had happened, whether she would be called on to try to convince her old friend that she hadn't been having an affair with her husband.

The day had seemed endless, one trauma after another. She glanced at Nathan, wishing he would speak to her, say anything to break the silence. But his back was still firmly turned to her. He seemed lost in thought, his shoulders tense. And when she turned again James was pushing through the doors, his face set in a scowl.

'I'll kill the rat!'

Olivia put her hand to her throat, her eyes panicky. 'Didn't he tell her? Wouldn't she believe him?'

'That's all taken care of.' His features relaxed. 'He told her—spilled a whole load of vitriol—going back to our childhood, his jealousy, his need to get back at me. And you, apparently, for giving him a succinct run-down on his character when he propositioned you. You never told me!' He put an arm round Olivia's shoulders and hugged her. 'It was his obvious spite that convinced Vanny he was telling the truth at last. But I could wring his neck for the damage he's done!'

'Then your wife's happy?' Nathan's voice was harsh. His eyes castigated both of them. 'I suggest you make sure she stays that way.' He strode to the doors. 'If he's done what I persuaded him to do, there's no longer any reason to stay. Coming, Olivia? Or would you prefer to be here?'

James began to say something but Olivia didn't stop to listen. Nathan was already striding through the reception area, as if he didn't care whether she left with him or not. She caught up with him just as he was unlocking the car door and he looked at her blankly, over the roof, as if he didn't know who she was.

Too close to torrents of tears to attempt to break the silence, Olivia felt herself begin to freeze inside. Somehow they were going to have to discuss their future. But there wasn't one, not for them; she was sure of that now.

He went straight upstairs as soon as they arrived home, brushing past her, not really seeing her, his face like stone.

Controlled aggression, Olivia thought bleakly, then made herself follow, her legs like lead.

He was packing, methodically folding things into an open suitcase.

'What are you doing?'

She knew the question was foolish. It was perfectly obvious what he was doing. Her voice sounded thick, not her own. Her whole body was beginning to shake. The gap between them was unbridgeable. She couldn't take in the speed with which it had all happened; the death of something that had been so beautiful had come so quickly, with such fearful finality.

'I'll move into a hotel,' he told her coolly, not raising his eyes to look at her, fastening the suitcase with a snap. 'I'll come back in a day or two for the rest of my things. I'll make sure I come while you're at work. As for the rest—the tedious details—' He made a short, dismissive gesture with his hand. 'We'll leave the solicitors to sort those out. You and your child will be taken care of.'

It was over. Somehow, stupidly, she had hoped against hope that they could find a way—

She leant weakly back against the door, closing her eyes, hiding the pain, the awful, unendurable, everlasting pain.

'It's your child too,' she whispered. She didn't know which was worse: the fact that he was walking out on her, going to a hotel—the one he had always used before, where he had Sasha Lee cosily installed?—or the fact that he was denying his own child.

'Let's not make a melodrama out of this.' His voice was different. She heard the rough edge of repression, of something savage held back, determinedly contained. 'It's over. I'm mature enough to cut my losses, get on with the rest of my life. Aren't you? After all, you must have known this would have to happen.'

He spoke as if their parting was inevitable, always had been, their days together numbered from the outset. Or from when the blonde bombshell had wiggled her way into his life? He had told her that his confession would hurt her. She knew she couldn't hurt more than she did at this moment.

Her bruised eyelids fluttered open, her violet eyes brilliant with unshed tears.

'Tell me why. How,' she demanded thickly, and watched his silver eyes narrow with impatience, saw him glance at his wristwatch, and flinched at the insult.

'Must we go through this?' he countered rawly. 'Chapter and verse?' He dragged air roughly into his lungs, his shoulders thrown back rigidly. 'The rot set in when we overheard what that low-life was saying. I'd never been jealous of anyone before in my entire life. The way I felt about James bloody Caldwell made me despise myself. I kept telling myself I was mistaken, that you had to have reasons for doing what you did—refusing to let me do anything about it in the first place, stopping the rumours at source, refusing to give up your job to be with me, running whenever he called, letting him kiss you...'

Olivia stared at him blankly. He was the one who was running out, going to another woman, and yet he was laying the blame on her! She simply couldn't take it in.

He bit out gratingly, 'You finally wiped the scales

from my eyes when you admitted, in front of the low-life, in front of me, that he'd been telling the truth all along, that you had, and still were having, an affair with James Caldwell.' He picked up his suitcase. 'Now, perhaps, we can lay it to rest, put it behind us.'

He was directly in front of her now, waiting to get out of the house, away from her, to forget he ever knew her. And he had got it all so wrong.

'No,' she said thickly, her throat tight with tension. 'No. James and I have never had an affair. He's my boss, my friend. Nothing else. I confessed to—to the other.' It was impossible to get the words out, but she knew she must. Her whole body trembled as she pushed the damning statement past her clenched teeth. 'I killed my first husband. I killed Max! That was the part that was true.'

The stark horror of that night swept over her remorselessly and she put up her hands, hiding her face. But Nathan dragged them away, his eyes probing her relentlessly.

'Do you know what you're saying?'

She nodded mutely, her teeth chattering, her face white.

'After it happened I went to pieces. I had a week off work. The—the funeral, and everything. When I got back I broke down. I tried not to. But I did. I told James everything—I—I guess Hugh must have overheard. James insisted I stay with him and Vanny for a while. I don't think I could have survived it without them. I owe them a huge debt of gratitude. Even if I had ever felt anything for James, apart from friend-ship—which I didn't—I would never have done anything about it. Never have done anything to hurt Vanny.'

She was shaking so much she could hardly stand. Wordlessly, Nathan picked her up and put her on the bed, wrapping the duvet round her shivering body. He left the room and reappeared moments later, a glass of brandy in his hand.

'Drink this.'

She shook her head, staring at the glass in his hand. At his fingers, strong and lean, fingers that had once touched her with adoration. He would never touch her again.

'I feel so guilty.' She looked at him despairingly. He held the glass to her lips, forcing her to drink. The fiery alcohol went straight to her head, making it spin, making her read compassion in the smoky grey eyes when she knew it couldn't exist.

He sat on the bed beside her, hitching the duvet higher around her. She didn't know why he was being so kind. Hadn't what she had confessed revolted him? Didn't he want to get right out of here, fly to the uncomplicated pleasures of Sasha's willing body?

'The only way to free yourself of the guilt is to make a full confession. To the authorities. Pay—' his voice shook slightly and then hardened '—pay the price. You must have had your reasons for doing what you did. I can't believe you would knowingly hurt another living soul, much less kill a man without extreme provocation. We'll sort this out together, hon, hire a first-class defence lawyer.'

She frowned, putting her fingers to her temples. Her head felt muzzy. 'The inquest—they brought in a verdict of accidental death. There wasn't a passenger air-bag, only a driver's, but if I'd been more in control—you know, concentrating properly—it wouldn't have happened. The other driver was coming straight at me. I had to swerve. But I needn't have gone into that wall.'

She began to sob, quietly, hopelessly, and he held her against his body, waiting, and when she was all cried out he said, the former tightness rolling out of his voice, 'He died in a road accident? Tell me about it. You've never said much about him, or his death. I didn't know if it was because you still missed him. I didn't want to force you to speak about your first marriage until you were ready. Tell me now.'

'We were totally unsuited,' she muttered into his shirt. She didn't know why he was holding her close, but she didn't want him to stop. It was like being back the way they were. The longer she could hold onto the illusion, the safer she would be.

'He swept me off my feet, as the saying goes. He was so full of life and enthusiasm. About a year into our marriage I realised it would never work. But I didn't give up. I'd married him, I had to stick with it. He kept starting up new businesses—stupid things—throwing our money into them and losing it. Looking back, I can see things could have been different, if I'd been different. I could have helped him, steered him away from the wilder enterprises, calmed him down. Heaven knows, one of the ventures might have paid off and he could have been the success he always wanted to be.'

She sniffed miserably. 'But not me!' Her voice

poured scorn on herself. 'I made up my mind that one of us had to be in steady, well-paid employment, and that it had to be me. I worked all the hours there were; it got so that we hardly saw each other. And then...' Her voice quavered, but she forced herself on. 'Just recently, I began to see parallels. The way I decided I'd stay and help James out, because I thought it was the right thing to do—regardless of what it was doing to us.'

She lifted her head, pushing her hair back from her face with shaky fingers. 'I was going to tell James that he'd have to do without me. I'm not indispensable. He could undo the damage Hugh had done to the firm without any help. You needed me more.' She felt his arms tighten around her. 'Only things went—went wrong.'

He'd met Sasha.

She tightened her mouth. She would not start to cry again. She would not! She couldn't meet his eyes; the look in them reminded her too sharply of all she had lost. She said brittly, 'You wanted to know how it ended. It was all my fault. If I'd been the type of wife, partner, he needed, things mightn't have gone so badly wrong. He'd met up with a woman who wrote self-help books. She persuaded him to set up a small publishing company. He thought it was a brilliant idea. He even mortgaged our home to raise funds.

'The first I heard of it was that evening. Late. He'd taken her out to dinner, to discuss the project, and phoned me from the restaurant to ask me to pick him up.' She drew in a long, shuddering breath and felt Nathan's arm tighten more firmly around her. 'I dropped his new business associate off at her flat. He'd wanted to drive but I hadn't let him. He'd had too much to drink.

'After we left her he told me about the mortgage, said he needed more than that to start up the project. He told me to ask James for a loan. I knew it would never get paid back; it would go down the drain the way everything else had gone,' she explained jerkily. 'I refused to do anything of the kind. He hit me.'

She did look at him then, her eyes haunted as she told him, 'He'd used violence before, early on in our marriage. He'd been pitifully sorry afterwards. So pathetic that I forgave him, but I warned him if he ever lifted a hand to me again I'd leave him.

'He never did, not until that night, but there was always the threat of it.' Her voice was a thin whisper in the silent room. 'Somehow, I kept control of the car. I should have stopped. Got out. Left him to it. But when he'd hit me something inside me had exploded. I knew he was drunk, that the violence that had always been just below the surface had broken loose—the air was thick with it—I could practically taste it!

'Yet I couldn't leave it. I told him I'd had enough, I was leaving him. I wasn't prepared to be a punch bag, there for him to take out his frustrations on. He hit me again. And I was reeling from it when that car came round a corner—and that was the end of his life.' She lifted her hands and covered her face, remorse in every line of her body. 'I can still see the crumpled car. They had to cut his body out. It was all my fault. Everything.'

'Sweetheart, don't torture yourself.' He lifted her hands from her face, cupping it between his own.

She looked at him with bewildered eyes. They were the words James had used, apart from the endearment. She didn't know why Nathan had used it. Unless he was sorry for her. She didn't want his pity.

'Max chose his own path. I doubt whether anything you could have done would have changed anything,' he said gently. 'All through your lives together he hurt you, he forced you to take responsibility for you both. You were so used to taking responsibility that you blamed yourself for his death. It was an accident and the way he hit you would have contributed to it. He killed himself. Believe me.'

She blinked, her lashes starred with tears. He brushed them softly away with his thumb, his own eyes misty as he repeated, 'Believe me, Livvy.'

She nodded, her eyes filling. She sucked her lower lip between her teeth and the weight of guilt fell from her shoulders. She did believe him.

He'd picked her overdeveloped sense of responsibility out of the tangled mess, pinpointing it, making her see the reason for the guilt she'd carried all these years, and, in seeing it, understanding it, he'd released it.

She gazed into the glowing depths of his eyes, her breath catching in her throat. She loved him so much. So very much. She almost said the words aloud but remembered just in time. She twisted her hands together in her lap, her spine straight.

'Thanks for listening. You don't know how much you've helped.' She pushed herself out of his arms,

up off the bed. It was time, she supposed numbly, to
say goodbye.

His arms came back round her, pulling her down
again. Then he reached forward, slipping her shoes
from her feet.

She didn't understand. 'What are you doing?'

'Taking care of you. It's past time someone did.'

'I can take care of myself.'

'So you've always said.' He grinned at her, the
beauty of it startling her, as it always did. Her poor
heart lurched with pain. 'So how come I don't believe
you?'

He was undoing the fastening of her skirt now. She
really couldn't take the torment of it. It reminded her
of happier times, loving times, perfect times. She
pushed his hands away. 'Weren't you going somewhere?'

'Only because I thought you'd confessed to having
an ongoing affair with James. I thought my world had
ended, that my worst nightmares were staring me in
the face. Now I'm staying right where I am, attending
to my wife.' Her skirt had finally gone, flung in a
corner. He was busily unbuttoning her blouse. 'I will
put you to bed and join you, and hold you close and
take care of you.'

'No! You can't! I won't let you!' She slapped his
fingers away. It was torture. She didn't want his pity;
she didn't want him caring for her, for one last night,
out of pity. 'You were going to that woman. Don't
let me make you keep her waiting!'

'What woman?' He paused in his renewed assault
on the buttons of her blouse, his head tilted as he

stared into her flushed, angry face. And then he
dragged in a heavy breath. 'Oh, Lord! Her! I'd forgotten!'

'My goodness, she will be pleased!' Olivia spat. 'I
expect she thinks she's unforgettable—how very awful for her to have to discover she's not!'

'Sweetheart!' he husked, pulling her resisting body
firmly into his arms. 'I had a confession to make.
Have a confession to make. God, this is going to
sound awful! I don't like myself much at this moment.
You're going to have to try to forgive me. Promise?'
he mumbled against her hair.

She made a half-hearted attempt to push him away,
then thought better of it, nuzzling closer instead, loving the way they felt together. If he had had a fling
with that busty blonde and regretted it, felt as awful
about it as he sounded, then she would forgive him.
She loved him too much to do anything other.

'Sasha Lee, the temp I hired in Hong Kong, is all
of fifty, happily married, with her first grandchild on
the way.'

'You barefaced liar!' Red in the face, she really
pushed at him, using all her strength. Was he asking
her to disbelieve the evidence of her own two eyes?

He didn't budge an inch.

'The Sasha Lee I introduced you to is an actress,
hired through an agency. I got the reprehensible idea
because you slammed the phone down on the real
thing that time. You were obviously jealous, thinking
I'd had a woman in my room all night. I'd left for
Hong Kong in a rotten mood because you'd agreed to
stay on with Caldwell. After you phoned and then

refused to speak to me I knew I couldn't bear to be away from you a second longer.

'I wrapped everything up and flew home, only to find you'd been away with James. When he dropped you off, kissed you, I thought I'd give you a taste of your own medicine. So I hired me a ''secretary'' and introduced you. I never set eyes on the woman again, apart from that evening when I employed her to trot downstairs as soon as she heard your key in the lock. I sent the cheque for her acting services to the agency. And that was that.'

She tipped her head back, staring into his eyes. 'What about the times she came here? Salad for lunch, for example? Don't forget the place reeked of her every time I got home.'

'I bought a bottle of the perfume she was using that night,' he confessed sheepishly. 'And splashed it all over the place when you were due home. I got to loathe the smell of it! Sweetheart, I love you so much—why should I so much as look at another woman?'

Tenderly, she put her hands on either side of his face, and then remembered exactly what had prevented him from making his confession before.

Unhappiness shadowed her eyes. 'The baby. Our baby. I know you wanted to plan our family, for some time in the future when you were willing to spend more time in one place. I let you down. It wasn't deliberate, I promise. What with one thing and another, I forgot to take my pills. Is it going to be a problem?'

For answer he rolled her back against the pillows,

his leg pinning her to the mattress as he gazed ador-
ingly into her face. 'The only problem is whether or
not you'll forgive me for my reaction. I was riven by
jealousy at the time, not thinking straight. Whenever
our children arrive they'll be truly welcome.'

He traced the line of her soft lips with the tips of
his fingers, his voice more serious now. 'In the past
I've always had to prove myself. Over and over. Once
wasn't enough. The best wasn't enough. I had to be
better than the best. Now the only thing I want is to
prove myself to you, prove my love for you. Make a
loving family with you, with you at the sweet warm
heart of it. And now I know there's nothing going on
between you and James you can stay on at work, with
my blessing, if that's what you really want.'

'For all that, my dearest love, I will forgive you
anything.' She reached for him, winding her arms
around his neck; there was naked hunger in his eyes.
She shook her head. 'Just for a month. I'll finish
working out my notice. Hugh had left him in a hole;
he'd been taking backhanders from our rivals, losing
us orders. James wanted me to help. I think he's quite
capable of doing it on his own. And after that I'll
work for you.' She smiled at him; he was her whole
world again, everything she had ever wanted or hoped
for. 'We're back to the way we were,' she sighed
blissfully, knowing it was the perfect truth.

'And we'll never leave it again,' he concurred, then
lingeringly covered her mouth with his.

'They could almost be twins,' Vanny remarked, her
doting eyes following the two dark-haired little boys

as they romped over the smooth green lawns.

'So they could.' Olivia's contented gaze followed their antics. James Caldwell the Second had been born seven months before her own precious Harry, but Harry had caught up. At two years old he was already slightly taller, slightly sturdier than his playmate. Already he was showing an encouraging resemblance to his drop-dead-gorgeous father.

Vanny flopped back on her sun lounger, her arms trailing over the sides. 'This is heaven. I keep telling James we need to move further out. London's fine, but the country's better for children. Another couple of hours and we'll be heading back unfortunately.'

'Make that at least three.' Olivia smiled, lifting her face to the warm rays of the afternoon sun. 'Angie and Edward are invited for tea, and you know how she talks!'

Nathan's parents had been delighted when they'd bought The Grange, even more so with the news that they were soon to become grandparents. And they made wonderful and willing baby-sitters when Nathan wined and dined his adored wife.

Just thinking about her wonderful husband, the life they shared, widened her smile to sheer ecstasy and she opened her eyes, finely tuned to his presence, as he and James walked up from the orchard where they'd been making a swing for the children.

The two men had become firm friends since the business of Hugh's malicious gossip had been resolved and, since Harry's birth, they had spent several companionable weekends here. Hugh, thankfully, was living permanently in Portugal, in partnership with some other dubious character, running a campsite and car-hire business. She didn't think he'd ever dare show his face in England again.

Olivia rose gracefully from her lounger and walked across the grass, passing James who was carrying the Second over to his supine mother. Harry, already mischievous and independent, was squealing and giggling, running away as fast as his sturdy little legs would carry him, pursued by Nathan who was making growly noises, pretending to try to catch him.

As soon as he saw Olivia he stopped, scooping the wriggling little boy up in his loving arms, his eyes soft as they lingered on her face, the fluid lines of her body beneath the skimpy blue sundress she was wearing. He used his free arm to hold her close to his lean body, dipping his dark head to taste her lips.

'You are more beautiful each day. More loved,' he murmured. 'You are my world.' He took a thick swath of her long dark hair and gently draped it around the three of them. 'Just the three of us, enclosed in our own perfect world.'

Harry giggled as the soft hair tickled his nose and Olivia said demurely, 'We're going to have to make room for one more.' She turned, taking his hand and placing it over her tummy. 'I only found out for sure this morning. I couldn't wait to tell you, but I wanted to wait until we were properly on our own.'

The radiant smile he gave her told her that she couldn't have brought him better news, and the barely contained passion of the kiss he gave her—somewhat hampered by Harry's demands for 'Me tiss too!' and

HARLEQUIN PRESENTS®

Psst. Pass it on...Harlequin Presents' exciting new miniseries is here!

Scandals!

You won't want to miss these scintillating stories of surprising affairs:

We've got your calendar booked!

Available wherever Harlequin books are sold.

From national bestselling author

SHARON SALA

SWEET BABY

So many secrets...

It happened so long ago that Tory Lancaster can't recall being the little girl who came home to an empty house.

A woman now, Tory is trying to leave behind the scarring emotions of abandonment and sorrow—desperate to love, but forever afraid to trust. With the help of a man who claims to love her, Tory is able to meet the past head-on—a past haunted by images of a mysterious tattooed man and the doll that was her only friend. But there are so many secrets, so little time....

Available in February 1998
at your favorite retail outlet.

**The Brightest Stars
in Women's Fiction.™**

MIRA

**Make a Valentine's date
for the premiere of**

◆ HARLEQUIN® **Movies**

starting February 14, 1998 with

Debbie Macomber's

This Matter of

Marriage

on

Just tune in to **The Movie Channel** the **second Saturday night** of every month at 9:00 p.m. EST to join us, and be swept away by the sheer thrill of romance brought to life. Watch for details of upcoming movies—in books, in your television viewing guide and in stores.

If you are not currently a subscriber to The Movie Channel, simply call your local cable or satellite provider for more details. Call today, and don't miss out on the romance!

*100% pure movies.
100% pure fun.*

◆ HARLEQUIN®
Makes any time special.™

KEY TO MY HEART

Unlock the secrets of romance just in time for the most romantic day of the year— Valentine's Day!

Key to My Heart
features three of your favorite authors,

Kasey Michaels,
Rebecca York
and Muriel Jensen,

to bring you wonderful tales of romance and Valentine's Day dreams come true.

As an added bonus you can receive Harlequin's special Valentine's Day necklace. FREE with the purchase of every *Key to My Heart* collection.

Available in January,
wherever Harlequin books are sold.

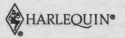

**Cupid's going undercover
this Valentine's Day in**

The Cupid Connection

Cupid has his work
cut out for him this
Valentine's Day with these
three stories about three
couples who are just too *busy*
to fall in love...well, not for long!

**ONE MORE VALENTINE
by Anne Stuart
BE MINE, VALENTINE
by Vicki Lewis Thompson
BABY ON THE DOORSTEP
by Kathy Gillen Thacker**

Make the Cupid Connection this February 1998!

Available wherever Harlequin and Silhouette books are sold.

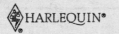 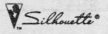

Don't miss these Harlequin favorites by some of our top-selling authors!